THE GUARDS

THE GUARDS

KEN BRUEN

ISIS

LARGE PRINT

Oxford

Copyright © Ken Bruen, 2001

First published in Great Britain 2001
by
Brandon
An imprint of Mount Eagle Publications

Published in Large Print 2011 by ISIS Publishing Ltd.,
7 Centremead, Osney Mead, Oxford OX2 0ES
by arrangement with
Brandon
An imprint of Mount Eagle Publications

British Library Cataloguing in Publication Data
Bruen, Ken.
    The guards.
    1. Taylor, Jack (Fictitious character) - - Fiction.
    2. Ex-police officers - - Ireland - - Galway - - Fiction.
    3. Galway (Ireland) - - Fiction.
    4. Detective and mystery stories.
    5. Large type books.
    I. Title
    823.9'14–dc22

ISBN 978–0–7531–5257–7 (hb)
ISBN 978–0–7531–5258–4 (pb)

Printed and bound in Great Britain by
T. J. International Ltd., Padstow, Cornwall

To
the Minister for Justice
from January 1993–December 1994

Special thanks to Vinny Brown, Charley Byrne's
Bookstore, Phyl Kennedy, Noel McGee

It's almost impossible to be thrown out of the Garda Síochána. You have to really put your mind to it. Unless you become a public disgrace, they'll tolerate most anything.

I'd been to the wire. Numerous

Cautions
Warnings
Last chances
Reprieves

And still I didn't shape up.

Or rather sober up. Don't get me wrong. The gardaí and drink have a long, almost loving relationship. Indeed, a teetotal garda is viewed with suspicion, if not downright derision, inside and outside the force.

My supervisor at the training barracks said,

"We all like a pint."

Nods and grunts from trainees.

"And the public likes us to like a pint."

Better and better.

"What they don't like is a blackguard."

He paused to let us taste the pun. He pronounced it, in the Louth fashion, "blaggard".

Ten years later I was on my third warning. Called before a supervisor, it was suggested I get help.

"Times have changed, sonny. Nowadays there's treatment programmes, twelve-step centres, all kinds of help. A spell in John O' God's is no shame any more. You'll rub shoulders with the clergy and politicians."

I wanted to say,

"That's supposed to be an incentive!"

But I went. On release, I stayed dry for a while, but gradually, I drank again.

It's rare for a garda to get a home posting, but it was felt my home town would be a benefit.

An assignment on a bitter cold February evening. Dark as bejaysus. Operating a speed trap on the outskirts of the city. The duty sergeant had stipulated,

"I want results, no exceptions."

My partner was a Roscommon man named Clancy. He'd an easygoing manner and appeared to ignore my drinking. I had a thermos of coffee, near bulletproof with brandy. It was going down easy.

Too easy.

We were having a slow duty. Word was out on our location. Drivers were suspiciously within the limit. Clancy sighed, said,

"They're on to us."

"Sure are."

Then a Mercedes blasted by. The clock hit thermo. Clancy shouted,

"Jaysus!"

I had the car in gear and we were off. Clancy, in the passenger seat, said,

"Jack, slow down, I think we might forget this one."

"What?"

"The plate . . . see the plate?"

"Yeah, so what."

2

"It's government."

"It's a bloody scandal."

I had the siren wailing, but it was a good ten minutes before the Merc pulled over. As I opened my door, Clancy grabbed my arm, said,

"Bit o' discretion, Jack."

"Yeah, right."

I rapped on the driver's window. Took his time letting it down. The driver, a smirk in place, asked,

"Where's the fire?"

"Get out."

Before he could respond, a man leaned over from the back, said,

"What's going on?"

I recognised him. A high profile TD. I said,

"Your driver was behaving like a lunatic."

He asked,

"Have you any idea who you're talking to?"

"Yeah, the gobshite who screwed the nurses."

Clancy tried to run block, whispered,

"Jeez, Jack, back off."

The TD was outa the car, coming at me. Indignation writ huge, he was shouting,

"Yah brazen pup, I'll have your job. Do you have any idea of what's going to happen?"

I said,

"I know exactly what's going to happen."

And punched him in the mouth.

UN-GUARDED

There are no private eyes in Ireland. The Irish wouldn't wear it. The concept brushes perilously close to the hated "informer". You can get away with most anything except "telling".

What I began to do was find things. Not a difficult task, it requires only patience and pig stubbornness. The latter was my strongest point.

I didn't come to one morning and shout, "God wants me to be a finder!" He could care less.

There's God and there's the Irish version. This allows Him to be feckless. Not that he doesn't take an interest, but He couldn't be bothered.

Because of my previous career, it was believed I had an inside track. That I knew how things worked. Over a period of time, people sought me out, asked for my help.

I hit lucky and found resolutions. A minor reputation began to build on a false premise. Most important of all, I was cheap.

Grogan's is not the oldest pub in Galway. It's the oldest unchanged pub in Galway.

While all the rest go

Uni-sex
Low-fat
Karaoke
Over-the-top

it remains true to the format of fifty or more years ago. Beyond basic. Spit and sawdust floor, hard seats, no-frills stock. The taste for

Hooches
Mixers
Breezers

hasn't yet been acknowledged.

It's a serious place for serious drinking. No bouncers with intercoms on the door. Not an easy pub to find. You head up Shop Street, skip Garavan's, turn into a tiny alley and you're home. If not free, at least unfettered.

I like it because it's the only pub that never barred me. Not once, not ever.

The bar is free of ornamentation. Two hurleys are criss-crossed over a blotched mirror. Above them is a triple frame. It shows a pope, St Patrick, and John F. Kennedy. JFK is in the centre.

The Irish saints.

Once the pope held centre field, but after the Vatican Council he got bounced. He clings to an outside left.

Precarious the pose.

I dunno which pope he is, but he has the look of them all. It's unlikely he'll regain mid-field any time soon.

Sean, the owner, who can recall Cliff Richard being young, said to me,

"Cliff was the English Elvis."

A horrendous concept.

Grogan's was my office. I sat there most mornings and waited for the world to come knocking. Sean would bring me coffee. A measure of brandy poured in — "to kill the bitterness".

Some days, he seems so frail I fear he'll never make the few steps to my table.

The cup rattles on the saucer like the worst of bad news. I'd say,

"Use a mug."

He'd be horrified, say,

"There are standards!"

Once I asked, as he shook in unison with the cup,

"Will you ever retire?"

"Will you ever stop drinking?"

Fair enough.

A few days on from Cheltenham, I was at my usual table. I'd won a few quid on the Champion Hurdle and hadn't yet squandered it. I was reading *Time Out*. Most every week I'd buy it. The London guide, listing nigh on every event in the capital.

My plan.

Oh yeah, I had one. Few things more lethal than a drinker with a plan. Here was mine.

I'd gather up every penny I had, borrow more, then head for London.

Rent a fine flat in Bayswater and wait.

That was it. Just wait.

This dream got me through many's the awful Monday.

Sean rattled over, put my coffee down, asked,

"Any sign of you going?"

"Soon."

He muttered some benediction.

Took a sip of my coffee and it burned the roof of my mouth.

Perfect.

The brandy after-hit lit among my gums, battering my teeth. Those moments before the fall.

Paradise encapsulated.

J.M. O'Neill in *Duffy is Dead* wrote that brandy gives you breath, then takes it away. More, you had to get up earlier and earlier to drink yourself sober enough for opening time.

Try explaining that to the non-afflicted.

A woman came in, looked round, then moved to the counter. I wished I was more than I was. Putting my head down, I tried out my detection skills. Or rather, my power of observation. Had only glanced at her; how much could I recall? A fawn medium-length coat, expensive cut. Brown hair to her shoulders. Make-up but no lipstick. Deep-set eyes over a button nose, strong mouth. Pretty, but not overly so. Sensible shoes of good brown leather.

Conclusion: out of my zone. She spoke to Sean, and he pointed at me. I looked up as she approached. She asked,

"Mr Taylor?"

"Yeah."

"May I have a few words?"

"Sure, sit down."

Up close, she was prettier than I'd seen. The lines around her eyes were deep. Her age I'd put at late thirties. I asked,

"Can I get you a drink?"

"The man is getting me coffee."

While we waited, she examined me. Not in a discreet fashion, openly without subterfuge. Sean came with the coffee . . . and behold, a plate of biscuits. I eyed him and he said,

"Mind yer business."

After he'd gone, she said,

"He's so fragile."

Without thinking, I said the worst thing,

"Him? He'll bury the both of us."

She flinched as if to duck. I stormed on,

"What do you want?"

Composing herself, she said,

"I need your help."

"How?"

"I was told you help people."

"If I can."

"My daughter . . . Sarah . . . she . . . she committed suicide in January. She was only sixteen."

I made appropriate noises of sympathy. She continued,

"I don't believe she'd . . . kill herself . . . she . . . just wouldn't."

I tried not to sigh. She gave a brief bitter smile, said,

"It's what a parent would say . . . isn't it? But, something happened after."

"After?"

"Yes, a man rang, said, 'She was drowned.'"

That threw me. I fumbled to get in gear, asked,

"What?"

"That's what he said. Nothing else, just those three words."

I realised I didn't even know her name.

"Ann . . . Ann Henderson."

How far behind was I lagging? Time to crank up. I bolted my laced coffee. Did something, said,

"Mrs Henderson . . . I . . ."

"It's not Mrs — I'm not married. Sarah's father lit out on us a long time ago. We only had each other . . . that's why she'd never . . . leave me . . . alone."

10

"Annie, when a tragedy like this happens, weirdos and cranks come out of the woodwork. It's a beacon to them. They ghoul-in on pain."

She bit her lower lip, then raised her head, said,

"He *knew*."

Rummaging in her bag, she produced a fat envelope, said,

"I hope there's enough there. It's the savings for our trip to America. Sarah had it all planned."

Next she laid a photograph beside the cash. I pretended to look. She said,

"Will you try?"

"I can't promise anything."

I know there were a lot of things I should, could, have said. But I said nothing. She asked,

"Why are you a drunk?"

Caught me blindside. I said,

"What makes you think I have a choice?"

"Ah, that's nonsense."

I was halfway angry, not all out but circling, asked,

"How come you want . . . a *drunk* . . . to help you?"

She stood up, gave me a hard look, said,

"They say you're good because you've nothing else in your life."

And she was gone.

" . . . responds quickly to the task at hand."

Assessment Report

I live by the canal. But a scarf away from the university. At night I like to sit, listen to the students roar.

And they do.

It's a small house, the old two-up, two-down. The landlord has converted it to two flats. I have the ground floor. A bank clerk named Linda is above. A country girl, she has adopted all the worst aspects of urban life. A sort of knowing cunning.

She's a looker, in her early twenties. Once, when she forgot her key, I picked the lock. Emboldened, I asked,

"Fancy an evening out?"

"Oh, I never break my golden rule."

"What's that?"

"Don't date drunkards."

Time later, her car had a flat and I changed the tyre. She said,

"Listen, that other time — I was outa line."

Outa line!

Everyone is quasi-American in the worst way.

I stood up, grease covering my hands, waited. She continued,

"I shouldn't have said, you know . . . the awful thing."

"Hey, forget it."

Forgiveness is a heady fix. It makes you stupid. I said,

"So, you want to go out, grab a bite?"

"Oh, I couldn't."

"What?"

"You're too old."

That evening, under darkness, I crept out, punctured her tyre again.

I read. I read a lot. Between bouts of booze, I get through some print. Mostly crime. Recently, I'd finished Derek Raymond's autobiography, *The Hidden Files*.

Class act.

He's the man.

That the drink had finally taken him out was a further bond. Over my bathroom mirror I'd placed his:

Existence is sometimes what a
forward artillery observer sees
of enemy lines through field glasses.
A distant and troubling view
brought suddenly into focus with a wealth of obscene
    detail.

It's the obscene detail I want to obliterate with every drink. But it's imprinted on my very soul, fetid and rank. No shaking it loose.

God knows I've tried; since the death of my father, I've fixated on death most days. I carry it, like a song, half-remembered.

A philosopher, Rochefoucauld, wrote that death is like the sun. No one can stare at it directly. I ploughed through books on death.

14

Sherwin Nuland — *How We Die*
Bert Keizer — *Dancing with Mister D*
Thomas Lynch — *The Undertaking*.
I dunno if I sought

        Answers
        Comfort
        Understanding.

I didn't get them.
A hole had opened in my gut that felt for ever raw. After the funeral, the priest said,

"The pain will pass."

I wanted to roar — "Fuck that, I don't want it to pass. I want to hug it to me lest I forget".

My father was a lovely man. As a child, I remember he'd suddenly clear all the furniture in the kitchen. The chairs, tables, piled against the wall. Then he'd take my mother's hand, and up and down the kitchen they'd dance. Laughter gurgling in her throat, she'd shout,

"Yah eejit."

No matter what was happening, he'd say,

"As long as you can dance, you're ahead."

He did for as long as he was able.

I never dance.

*"Dead children do not give
us memories,
they give us dreams."*

Thomas Lynch, *The Undertaking*

I visited the grave of the dead girl. She was buried in Rahoon Cemetery. Where Nora Barnacle's dead lover lies.

I can't explain why I wanted to touch base there. My father's grave rests on the small hill. I was too ragged to say hello. Felt as if I was sneaking past. There are those days I feel his loss too sharply to say hello.

Sarah Henderson's plot was down near the east wall. It's one of the few spots to catch the sun. A makeshift, temporary cross read:

SARAH HENDERSON

Nothing else.
I said,
"Sarah, I'll do what I can."
Outside the gates I found a phone box, called Cathy B. She answered on the ninth ring with
"What?"
"Whoa, Cathy . . . nice phone manner."
"Jack?"
"Yeah."
"How are you?"
"I'm at the cemetery."
"Better than *in*."
"Can you do some work?"
"Oh yeah, like I need the bread, so totally."

17

I gave her the background, the details, said,
"Talk to her school friends, boyfriend . . ."
"Don't tell me my job."
"Sorry."
"You should be. I'll call in a few days."
Click.

About a year ago, I was heading home late along the canal. It's a happening place after midnight. Drinking school, dopers, eco-warriors, ducks, and the no-frills crazies. I fit right in.

A non-national offered to sell me his coat, but otherwise it was uneventful. As I got to the end of the canal, I saw a girl on her knees before a man. For one illucid moment, I thought he was getting a blow job. Until I saw his hand go up, come crashing down on her head. I came behind, used my elbow to hit him on the neck.

He fell against the railing. The girl's face was cut, and bruising already showed on her cheek. I helped her up. She said,

"He's going to kill me."

I elbowed him again and he went,

"Urg . . . gh."

I said,

"I don't think so."

I asked her,

"Can you walk?"

"I'll try."

I grabbed the guy by his shirt.

Up

One

Two

And over.

Let his own weight launch him into the canal.

As I was opening the door to my flat, we could hear roars from the water. She said,

"I don't think he can swim."

"Who cares?"

"Not me."

I made tower-block hot whiskeys.

> Tons of sugar
> Cloves
> Gallon of Jameson.

Put the glass in her two hands, said,

"Get that in yah."

She did.

I put Lone Star on the speakers, kicking off with "Amazed". She said,

"Is that Country and Western?"

"Sure is."

"It's shite."

"Drink up, you won't care."

I took a full look at her. Spiked hair, pierced eyebrow, trowel-thick black make-up. Somewhere in there was a pretty girl. Her age could be sixteen or thirty-six. Her accent was London, blunted a little by Irish inflexion. The effect was as if she was for ever about to launch into what the English believe is a brogue.

That she never did is to her ever-lasting credit.

No wonder I liked her.

A marathon of heavy silver bracelets lined her left arm. Didn't quite hide the old tracks. I said,

"You were on the gear."

"What are you, the Old Bill?"

"Used to be."

"You what?"

"I used to be a cop."

"Bleedin' hell."

That's how I met Catherine Bellingham. She'd washed up in Galway in the wake of a rock group who played the Black Box. They split, she stayed.

"I sing," she said.

Without preamble, she launched into "Troy". Unaccompanied, it must be the most difficult choice. I had never been an avid Sinead O'Connor fan but, hearing this, I reconsidered.

Cathy made it a dirge of bleak beauty. I was astonished, held my drink up to the light.

"This is powerful shit."

Immediately, she followed with "A Woman's Heart".

Yeah, Mary Black would also require reassessment.

It was like I'd never heard those songs. After, I said,

"Christ, you're good."

"I am, amn't I?"

I poured more drink, said,

"Here's to beauty."

She didn't touch hers, said,

"I never do the next song, but I'm drunk so . . ."

It was "No Woman, No Cry".

I'm an alky, I was born to these sentiments. Listening to her, I wished I had the strongest Colombian available. Conversely, it made me feel I had a shot. But at what I didn't know. Cathy stopped, said,

"That's it, show's over."

I said, without considering,

"No people sing with such pure voices as those who live in deepest hell."

She nodded, said,

"Kafka."

"Who?"

"He said that."

"You know him?"

"I've known hell."

KEENING

In Ireland they say, "If you want help, go to the guards — if you don't want help, go to the guards."

I went.

Since my dismissal, every few months, I'd receive the following letter:

THE DEPARTMENT OF JUSTICE

A Chara,

In compliance with the terms of your termination, it is required you surrender all property belonging to the Government.

See Article 59347A of Uniform and Equipment. It has come to our attention you have failed to return Item 8234 — A regulation garda all-weather coat.

We trust in your speedy return of said item.

Mise le meas,

B. Finnerton.

I crumpled the most recent and lobbed it across the room. I missed. The rain was bucketing down outside as I bundled into Item 8234.

Fit like harmony.

The only link I had to my former career.

Would I return it? Would I fuck.

★ ★ ★

My former colleague, Clancy from Roscommon, had risen through the ranks. I stood outside the garda barracks and wondered at my welcome.

Taking a deep breath, I headed in. A garda, aged about twelve, asked,

"Yes, sir?"

Jesus, how old had I got. I said,

"Would it be possible to see Garda Clancy? I'm not sure of his rank."

The youngster's eyes popped. He said,

"Superintendent Clancy?"

"Must be."

Then suspicion.

"Have you an appointment?"

"Tell him Jack Taylor is here."

He considered, then,

"I'll check. Wait here."

I did.

Read the notice board. Made the gardaí appear a friendly, laid-back outfit. I knew better. The youngster returned, said,

"The superintendent will see you in Interview Room B. I'll buzz you through."

He did.

The room was painted bright yellow. A lone table, two chairs. I sat in the suspect's one. Wondered whether to remove my coat, but they might seize it. Left it on.

The door opened, Clancy entered. A whole different animal from the man of my memory. He'd become, as they say, stout. Like fat, as in very. As no doubt fits a super. His face was ruddy, jowled, sagging. He said,

"By the holy."

I stood up, said,

"Superintendent."

Pleased him. He said,

"Sit, man."

I did.

We took time out, to survey, assess. Neither of us hot on what we got. He asked,

"What can I do for you, boyo?"

"Just a little information."

"Oh."

I told him about the girl, her mother's request. He said,

"I heard you'd become some sort of half-arsed private dick."

I'd no reply, so nodded. He said,

"I'd have expected more of you, Jack."

"Than what?"

"Leeching off a poor woman's grief."

That hurt 'cause of how close to the truth it was. He shook himself, said,

"I remember the case. It was suicide."

I mentioned the phone call, and he gave a disgusted sigh, said,

"You probably made that call yerself."

I gave my last try, asked,

"Could I see the file?"

"Don't be a complete eejit . . . and sober up."

"Is that a 'no'?"

He stood, opened the door, and I grappled for some brilliant exit line. None came. As I waited to be buzzed out, he said,

"Don't become a nuisance, Jack."

"I'm already that."

I headed for Grogan's. Consoled myself they hadn't got my coat. Sean was behind the counter, asked,

"Who ate your cake?"

"Fuck off."

I stormed to my usual seat, plonked down. After a bit, Sean arrived with a pint and a chaser, said,

"I presume you're still drinking."

"I've been working . . . OK?"

"On the case?"

"What else?"

"God help that poor woman."

Later, the drink in full sway, I said to Sean,

"Sorry if I was a bit touchy."

"A bit?"

"Pressure, it's pressure I don't do well."

He blessed himself, said,

"Oh, thank God! Is that all it is?"

*"When did a private detective
solve a crime?
Never!"*

Ed McBain

Some people live their lives as if they were in a movie. Sutton lives his as if he were in a bad movie.

It's said the difference between one friend and none is infinity. I'll buy that. Or that no man who has a friend can be considered a failure. I have to buy that.

Sutton is my friend. As a young garda, I'd pulled border duty. It's a tedious assignment of rain and more rain. You longed for a shoot-out. What you got was cold sausage and chips in a Nissan hut.

Recreation was the pub.

I drank in the imaginatively titled The Border Inn. My first call there, the barman said,

"You're the heat."

I laughed out loud, close to frostbite as I was. He said,

"I'm Sutton."

He looked like Alex Ferguson. Not a young version but the shouting showman of treble glory days.

"Why are you a guard?" he asked,

"To annoy my father."

"Ah, hate the old man, do you?"

"No, I love him."

"You're just confused, is it?"

"It was a test, see if he'd try to stop me."

"Did he?"

"No."

"Well, you can pack it in then."

"I kinda like it now."

Over the months of my border duty, I drank in Sutton's solidly. One time, we went to a dance in South Armagh, I'd asked Sutton,

"What will I need?"

"An Armalite."

En route to the dance, I was wearing Item 8234 and Sutton asked,

"Tell me you'll take the coat off for the dance?"

"Maybe."

"Oh, another thing. Don't talk."

"What?"

"This is bandit country; your soft vowels could land us in it."

"How am I supposed to dance — slip them a note?"

"Jesus, Taylor, it's a dance. We're going to drink."

"I could show them my truncheon."

The night was a disaster. A dance hall packed with couples. Not an unattached woman anywhere. I said to Sutton,

"They're all paired off."

"Sure this is the North, you can't be too careful."

"Couldn't we just have gone to a pub?"

"And miss the ambiance?"

The band were sub-showband era. Nine guys in blue blazers, white pants, and more bugles than the army.

Any army.

Their repertoire went from the Hucklebuck through Eurovision favourites to crescendo with the Beach Boys.

You don't know hell till you stand in a damp dance hall in South Armagh as the crowd sing along to "Surfing Safari".

On the way back, Sutton was navigating a treacherous road when I spotted headlights in the mirror. I said,

"Uh-uh."

The car made various attempts to overtake, but Sutton was having none of it. We finally shook them off near the border. I asked,

"Which side do you think that was?"

"The bad side."

"Which is . . ."

"The one that follows you at four in the morning."

What remains isn't always
the worst
that's left behind.

Sutton moved to Galway. I asked,

"Are you following me?"

"You betcha."

He decided to be an artist. I said,

"Piss artist more like."

But he had talent. I dunno was I delighted or jealous. Both probably, feeding off each other in the Irish fashion. His canvases began to sell, and he decided to act artistic. Bought a cottage in Clifden. Truth be told, I thought he'd become a complete asshole.

Told him so.

He laughed, said,

"It's only a pose; like happiness, it won't last."

Nor did it.

He was back to his old self in a few months. Galway rain will drown out near most pretensions.

Sutton at his worst was better than most people at their best.

After my meeting with Clancy I rang Sutton, said,

"Help."

"What's happening, dude?"

"The guards!"

"That crowd. What are they doing?"

"They won't help me."

"Get on yer knees and thank God."

I arranged to meet him at Grogan's. When I arrived, he was deep in conversation with Sean. I said,

"Guys!"

Sean straightened up. No mean feat. His vertebrae howled in anguish at the effort. I said,

"You need Radox."

"I need a blooming miracle."

Then they both looked expectantly towards me. I said,

"What?"

In unison, they said,

"Notice anything new?"

I looked round. Same old pub, the line of sad solid drinkers at the counter, chained to their pints by dreams no longer relevant. I shrugged. Which is not an easy thing to pull off for a man of forty-five years. Sean said,

"Yah blind hoor, look where the hurleys used to be."

A Sutton painting. I moved closer. It appeared to be a blonde girl standing on a deserted street. Equally, it could have been Galway Bay. One of the drinkers said,

"I preferred the hurleys."

Sean said,

"Gifted, isn't it?"

He bustled off to make our coffee

Laced

And

Unlaced.

"I had an exhibition at Kenny's. That one was priced at five hundred guineas."

"Guineas!"

"Yeah, you can't beat the touch of class. Like it?"

"Is it Galway Bay?"

"It's *The Blonde on the Street Corner*."
"Oh . . ."
"Crime novel written in 1954 by David Goodis."
I put up my hand, said,
"Let's have the workshop later."
He grinned, said,
"You're a thick bollix."
I told him about my new case. He said,
"The rate of Irish teenage suicide has soared."
"I know, I know, but something about the call the mother got . . ."
"Another sicko."
"You're probably right."
Later, we walked down Shop Street. A Romanian woman was playing a tin whistle outside Eason's. Well, she was blowing into it intermittently. I went over, gave her a few bob. Sutton exclaimed,
"Christ, you're only encouraging her."
"I paid her to stop."
She didn't.
An eco-warrior was outside Anthony Ryan's, juggling flaming torches. He dropped one but seemed unfazed. A garda was ambling towards us. Sutton nodded to him and the garda saluted us.
"Men."
Sutton gave me a curious look, asked,
"Do you miss it?"
I knew what he meant but asked,
"Miss what?"
"The guards."
I didn't know, said,

"I dunno."

We went into Kenny's in time to clock a bad shoplifter put a Patrick Kavanagh down his pants. Des, the owner, glided past, said,

"Put it back."

He did.

We passed through the ground floor, out to the gallery. Two of Sutton's canvases were on show, sold stickers prominent. Tom Kenny said,

"You're making waves."

Which is as high as praise rises. I said to Sutton,

"You can pack in the day job."

"What day job?"

Hard to say which of us liked that answer best.

The next few days were spent investigating. Tracking down any witnesses to the "suicide". There were none. Talked to the girl's teacher, school friends, and learnt precious little. Unless Cathy B. found startling evidence, the case was over.

Friday night, I resolved to have a quiet time. Two pints and a chips carry-home. Alas, the pints got away from me and I hit the top shelf. Black Bush, too many to recall. I did get the chips. Piece of cod thrown in to make it appear substantial.

Is there anything more comforting than doused-in-vinegar chips. The smell is like the childhood you never had. As I approached my flat, I was in artificial contentment. Turning to my door, the first blow caught me on the neck. Then a kick to the cobblers. For mad reasons, I hung on to the chips. Two men, two big men. They gave me a highly professional hiding. A mix of kicks and punches that came with a rhythm of precision. Without malice but with absolute dedication. I felt my nose break. Would swear it made the "crunch" sound. One of them said,

"Get his hand, spread the fingers."

I fought that.

Then my fingers were splayed on the road. It felt cold and wet. Twice the shoe came down. I roared for all I was worth.

They were done.

The other said,

"Won't be playing with himself for a bit."

A voice close to my ear.

"Keep your nose out of other people's business."

I wanted to cry, "Call the guards."

As they headed off, I tried to say, "Buy your own chips," but my mouth was full of blood.

those moments before the close . . .

Four days I was in and out of fever at University College Hospital, Galway; locals still call it "The Regional". If you were there, you were fucked. Now if you're there, you're lucky.

A woman from the old neighbourhood said,

"One time we'd stomachs but no food. Now we have food and no stomachs."

Or

"Loveen, there's no drying out. When we had great drying, we'd no clothes."

Argue that.

I came to and an Egyptian doctor was checking my file. I asked,

"Cairo?"

He gave a dry smile, said,

"You return to us, Mr Taylor."

"Not voluntarily."

I could hear the hospital radio. Gabrielle with "Rise".

I'd have hummed "Knocking on Heaven's Door" with her backing band but my mouth was swollen. When she returned to music, I read her ex-boyfriend's stepfather's head was found in a tip in Brixton.

I'd have shared this with the doctor but he'd gone. A nurse entered and began immediately fluffing my pillows. They do this if there's the vaguest hint of you getting comfortable.

My left hand was heavily bandaged. I asked,

"How many broken?"

"Three fingers."

"My nose?"

She nodded, then said,

"You've a visitor; feel up to it?"

"Sure."

I'd expected Sutton or Sean. It was Ann Henderson. She gasped on seeing me. I said,

"You should see the other guy."

She didn't smile. Moved up close and said,

"Is this my fault?"

"What?"

"Is it because of Sarah?"

"No . . . no . . . course not."

She put a paper bag on the locker, said,

"I brought you grapes."

"Any chance of Scotch?"

"That's the last thing you need."

Sean appeared in the doorway, went,

"By the holy."

Ann Henderson leant over, kissed my cheek, whispered,

"Don't drink."

And was gone.

Sean fragiled towards me, saying,

"You must have pissed someone off big time."

"It's what I do."

"Did anyone call the guards?"

"They were the guards."

"You're coddin'."

"I saw their shoes, at closer range than I wanted. They were the boys all right."

"Jesus!"

He sat down, looking worse than I felt. Then put a Dunnes' bag on the bed, said,

"Things I thought you'd need."

"Any drink?"

I felt like the mad priest in "Father Ted". I rummaged through the bag.

> 6 oranges
> Lucozade
> Box of Milk Tray
> Deodorant
> Pyjamas
> Rosary beads

I held up the beads, asked,

"How bad did you hear I was?"

He reached into his jacket, produced a half of Jameson. I said,

"God bless you."

I drank it from the bottle, felt it move my shattered nose. Bounced against my heart and pounded along my sore ribs. I gasped,

"Mighty."

Sean nodded off. I shouted,

"Shop."

And he jumped. Seemed lost and worse, old. He said,

"The heat, Christ . . . why do they have these places like ovens?"

Maybe the painkillers helped, but I felt absolutely pissed, asked,

"Where's Sutton?"

Sean looked away and I said,

"What? . . . come on."

He lowered his head, mumbled. I said,

"Speak up . . . I hate when you do that."

"There was a fire."

"Oh God!"

"He's okay, but the cottage is gone. All his paintings too."

"When?"

"The same. Same night you got hammered."

I shook my head. Bad idea as the whiskey sloshed behind my eyes. I said,

"What the hell's going on?"

The doctor reappeared, said,

"Mr Taylor, it's important you rest."

Sean stood up, laid his hand on my shoulder.

"I'll be back tonight."

"I won't be here."

I swung my legs out of bed. The doctor, alarmed, said,

"Mr Taylor, I must insist you get back into bed."

"I'm leaving . . . ADA . . . isn't it?"

"ADA?"

"Against the doctor's advice. Jeez, don't you watch ER?"

I had a moment's dizziness, but the booze rode shotgun. My blood sang out for creamy pints of

Guinness. A whole shitpile of them. Sean had the trouble of the world on his face, said,

"Jack, be reasonable."

"Reasonable! I was never that."

I consented to a cab, and as I was wheelchaired to the exit, a nurse said,

"Yah big eejit."

GREAT SHINERS

The nun was reading Patricia Cornwell. She saw me glance at the cover, said,

"I prefer Kathy Reichs."

There's no answer to this. No polite answer anyway. I asked,

"Am I too early?"

She reluctantly put her book aside, said,

"There's half an hour yet. You could walk round the grounds."

I did.

The Poor Clare Convent is smack in the centre of the city. Every Sunday, at 5.30, there's a Latin mass. It's like a throwback to fifty years before.

Downright medieval.

The ritual, the smell of incense, the Latin intonations are a comfort beyond articulation.

I dunno why I go. Ask me for belief and I reach for the racing page. In an unguarded moment, I told Cathy B. She'd been plaguing me ever since. I said,

"Why? You're some kind of English heathen."

"I'm a Buddhist."

"Jeez, see what I mean? Why on earth would you want to go?"

"It's so *Brideshead*."

"What?"

"In England, High Catholicism is for the special few. Evelyn Waugh, Graham Greene, all converted."

She wore me down. I watched now as she turned into the convent. I'd warned,

"Dress appropriately. None of that Goth trip."

Now she was wearing a full-length dress. Fine for a dress dance at the Bank of Ireland, but mass! Then I saw the Doc Martens. I said,

"Docs!"

"I polished them."

"But they're blue."

"Nuns do blue."

"How would you know?"

"I saw *Agnes of God*."

Then she saw my nose, my fingers in the cast, raised her eyebrows. I told her. She said,

"Wow, like cool."

"What?"

"Think they'll come after me?"

"There isn't a 'they' . . . it's coincidence."

"Yeah . . . sure."

The bell rang. Cathy asked,

"How will I know what to do?"

"Do what I do."

"That's bound to get us slung out."

Inside, the tiny church was warm and welcoming. Cathy grabbed a hymn sheet, squeaked,

"There's singing."

"Not for you."

But it was.

The congregation joined in the song performance. Cathy loudest of all. A nun came up after to congratulate her, asked,

"Would you like to sing some Sunday?"

I hopped in.

"She's not one of us."

Cathy and the nun gave me a look of withering contempt. I slunk outside.

Fr Malachy had arrived. No sooner off his bicycle than he lit a cigarette. I said,

"You're late."

He smiled, answered,

"But for what?"

Malachy was like Sean Connery, minus

The tan

The golf.

You couldn't call him a friend. Priests have other loyalties. I knew him since I was a child. He took in my injuries, said,

"You're still drinking."

"This was unrelated."

He took out his cigarettes. Major. The green and white packet. As strong as a mule kick and twice as lethal. I said,

"You're still smoking."

"Me and Bette Davis."

"She's dead."

"My point exactly."

He watched two nuns and said,

"Great shiners."

"What."

"Polishing. No one can touch them for it."

I looked round then asked,

"Where's the Church on suicide these days?"

"Leaving us, are yah?"

"I'm serious. Is it still the 'can't be buried in hallowed ground' stance?"

"Ah, you're very out of touch, Jack."

"That's an answer?"

"No, that's a sad fact."

FACTS

Cathy B. and I were literally "eating out". At the Spanish Arch, with Chinese takeaway, watching the water. She said, "I have my report."

"Let's finish the grub first."

"Sure."

I threw some chow mein to the swans. They didn't appear to like it much. A wino approached, asked,

"Gis a fiver."

"I'll give you a quid."

"Long as it's not a Euro."

He eyed the food and I offered him mine. With great reluctance he took it, asked,

"Is it foreign?"

"Chinese."

"I'll be hungry again in an hour."

"But you have the quid."

"And my health."

He ambled off to annoy some Germans. They took his photo. Cathy said,

"Before my report, can I tell you a story?"

"I can do stories."

She launched.

"My dad was a second-rate accountant. You know the old joke . . . 'How can you tell an extrovert accountant? He looks at *your* shoes.' Anyway, he worked without promotion till he was fifty. My mother nagged him ferociously. What I remember most is he

52

had ten suits. All identical and the object of my mother's wrath. She was, to quote the Irish, 'a holy terror'.

"He always treated me with kindness and generosity. When I was nine, he lost his job due to drink. My mother ordered him out. He took his ten suits and went to live under Waterloo Station. In the tunnels there, he'd put on a fresh suit, and when it was dirty, he threw it away. At his last one, he stepped under the 9.05 from Southampton.

"The express.

"I hated him 'cause my mother did. Then, when I understood who *she* was, I began to comprehend him. I once read that Hemingway's mother sent him the gun which his father used to kill himself. My mother would never have gone in for studied viciousness. After her death, I had to clear out her things. I found a train timetable for arrivals at Waterloo. Perhaps she thought he'd finally come up to speed."

She was crying, the tears rolling down her face and hitting the curried noodles with a soft plink, like rain off a sheet of glass. I opened our lone bottle of wine, handed it over. She waved it away, said,

"I'm okay. Are you still techno ignorant?"

"I am."

"I'll keep it simple. I fed a number of items into the computer, teenage suicides over the past six months, and got two hits. Ever hear of Planter's?"

"Who make peanut butter?"

"No, it's a massive DIY shop at the rear of Edward Square."

"Where the new Dunnes is?"

"Yes."

"Jeez, Edward Square! I mean . . . come on. In the middle of Galway, how Irish is that?"

She gave me a look, then continued.

"Of three suicides, three of the girls worked part-time there."

"So?"

"So it's strange. The owner, Bartholomew Planter, is a transplanted Scot. Rich as the lottery."

"It's a reach, Cathy."

"There's more."

"Go on."

"Guess who protect the premises."

"I dunno."

"Green Guard."

"And?"

"They employ moonlighting guards."

"Oh."

"Oh is right."

She took the wine, drank, asked,

"What now, hot shot?"

"Maybe I'll go see Mr Planter."

"Mr Ford."

"Ford?"

"He runs the place."

"Well, I'll go see him then."

She watched the water for a time, then,

"Wanna fuck?"

"What?"

"You heard."

54

"Jeez, you're all of what . . . nineteen?"

"Are you going to pay me for my work?"

"Am . . . soon."

"So, at least let me get laid."

I stood up, said,

"Anything else?"

"Of course."

"Well."

"Mr Planter likes to play golf."

"I don't think that falls under suspicious behaviour."

"It does if you know who he plays with."

"Who?"

"A Superintendent Clancy, that's who."

I walked away.

D I Y

I was going to say that I put on my best suit but I only have one. Bought in Oxfam two years ago. It's dark blue with narrow lapels. Makes me look like a wide boy. Remember the Phil Collins video where there's three of him. That's the suit. I can only pray it doesn't make me look like Phil Collins. If I say it was less than a tenner, you get the idea.

Course, that was before Oxfam got notions. I had a white shirt that unfortunately I washed with a navy t-shirt. I act like this is an accessorised outfit. A tie, loosened to give the "Mister, I don't give a fuck" effect. Solid brown brogues. The shoe maketh the man. Spit shined till you could see your reflection.

Checked myself in the mirror. Asked,

"Would you buy a car from this man?"

No.

I had a mobile phone number for Sutton and rang that. Got the answering service and left a message. Walking into town I tried to feel like a citizen. Couldn't quite pull it off. At the abbey, I went in and lit a candle to St Anthony, the finder of lost things. It crossed my mind to ask him to find myself, but it seemed too theatrical. People were going to confession, and how I wished I could seek such a cleansing.

Outside, a Franciscan bid me good morning. He was the picture of robust good health. My age, without a line in his face. I asked,

"Do you like your work?"

"God's work."

Served me right for asking. I continued on to Edward Square. Walked through Dunnes and saw six shirts I couldn't afford. On through to Planter's. It was big. Covered the whole of what used to be a parking lot. At reception I asked if I could see Mr Ford. The girl asked,

"Have you an appointment?"

"No."

"I see."

But she didn't. She rang his office and he agreed to meet me. I took the elevator to the fifth floor. His office was modest and he was on the phone. Hand waved me to a chair. He was small, bald, with an Armani suit. An air of controlled energy from him. Finishing the call, he turned to me. I said,

"Thank you for seeing me. I'm Jack Taylor."

He gave a brief smile. Small yellow teeth. Flash suit and bad teeth. The smile had no connection to warmth. He said,

"You say that name as if it means something. It means zero to me."

I could smile too. Show him what Ultra-Brite might achieve, said,

"I'm investigating the death of Sarah Henderson."

"Are you a policeman?"

"No."

"Have you any official standing?"

"Zero."

Nice to hop the word back. He said,

"So, I have no obligation whatsoever to talk to you?"

"Save common decency."

He walked round the desk, adjusted the razor crease in his trousers, sat on the edge of the desk. His feet didn't quite reach the floor. His shoes were Bally. I know so well what I can't afford. Argyll socks with a snazzy pattern. He said,

"There's no good reason not to sling your sorry ass on out of here."

I realised the guy loved to talk, no sound so sweet as his own voice. I said,

"Would you be surprised to hear three girls, now dead, all worked here?"

He slapped his knee, said,

"Have you any idea of the hundreds of staff we put through our doors? I'd be amazed if they all lived for ever."

"Did you know the girl?"

I don't think I knew what sardonic really meant till I heard him laugh, he said,

"I very much doubt it."

"Would you check, as a favour to the girl's mother?"

He hopped off the desk, hit the intercom, said,

"Miss Lee, rustle up the file on a Sarah Henderson."

He sat down, the portrait of relaxation. I said,

"That's impressive."

"An intercom?"

"No, how you didn't even have to think for a second to get the girl's name."

"It's why I'm sitting here in a suit worth three grand and you're . . . shall we say . . . in last year's remainder."

The secretary arrived with a thin folder. Ford reached
for glasses, pince-nez, naturally. Made a series of

M . . . m . . .'s

Hm . . . m . . .

Ahh's . . .

Then closed the file, said,

"The girl was a shirker."

"A what?"

"Work shy. We had to let her go."

"That's it?"

"Indeed. She was, alas, what we call a reject. No
future whatsoever."

I stood up, said,

"You're right about that. She certainly has no future."

. . . so smug believed — that desolation
had the limits full explored.

Sutton was staying in the Skeff. Like every place else in Galway, it had recently been renovated. Any space is immediately seized for "luxury apartments".

I found Sutton at the bar, nursing a pint of Guinness. Inspired, I said,

"Hey."

He didn't answer, took in my vaguely healing injuries, nodded. I took a stool beside him, signalled to the barman for two pints, said,

"Remember Cora?"

Head shake and

"I'm not from here, remember."

The pints came and I reached to pay, but Sutton said,

"Put it on the slate."

"You've a slate?"

"Comes with being an artist . . . a burnt-out artist in fact."

I thought it was best to take it head-on, said,

"My hiding, your blaze, I didn't believe they were connected. Or connected to anything else."

"And now?"

"I think it's all deliberate. I'm . . . sorry . . ."

"Me too."

Silence then till he said,

"Run it all by me."

I did.

Took longer than I thought, and the slate grew. When I'd finished, he said,

"Bastards."

"Worse than that."

"Can you prove anything?"

"Nothing."

I told him about Green Guard, the security firm, said,

"They employ the guards."

"They do. And you're thinking . . . what?"

"See if my assailants are there."

"Then?"

"Payback."

"I like that. Include me in."

"I'd like to meet Mr Planter too. He or Ford killed that girl. I want to know how and why."

"Planter's a rich fuck."

"Oh yeah."

"Probably got notions."

"Sure to."

He took a large swig. It left a white foam moustache. He asked,

"Think he likes paintings?"

"Oh yeah."

"Lemme work on that."

"Great."

"Want to grab some grub or just get wrecked?"

"Wrecked sounds better."

"Barman!"

. . . fears daily revealing . . .
Real
The lines on hour
Scarred.

Next day, I was dying. Not your run-of-the-mill hangover but the big enchilada. The one that roars — SHOOT ME!

I surfaced near noon. Events up till four the previous afternoon were retrieveable. Napalm after that. I do know Sutton and I ended up in O'Neachtain's.

Glimpses peeked through:

> Line dancing with Norwegians.
> Arm wrestling the bouncer.
> Double Jack Daniels.

My clothes were crumpled near the window. The remains of late night takeaway peering from under a chair. Trod on chips and what appeared to be an off-green wing of chicken.

Christ!

Did some serious throwing up. Morning prayer. Old establishment ritual, on my knees before the toilet bowl.

Twyfords!

They built bowls to endure.

Finally, purged, my system settled into a rhythm of spasmodic retching. The kind that tries to vacuum your guts up through the thorax. Thorax. Good word that. Gives a feeling of medical detachment.

I wanted the hair of the dog. Jeez, I wanted the whole dog. But it would lead to more lost days. I had vengeance to wreak, villains to catch. With trembling hands I tried to roll a joint. Sutton had given me some "waccy-baccy", said,

"From the Blue Atlas Mountains, this is serious shit. Treat with respect."

Couldn't roll the spiff. Went to the cupboard, found a stale cherry muffin. Scraped the guts out. Heated the hash in tinfoil then poured liberally into the cake. Popped the mess in the micro-wave and blitzkrieged.

Boy, it looked a sorry sight. After it cooled, I tried a bite. Hey, not bad. Between tentative sips of water, I got it down.

Then sat back, see where it went.

Orbit.

Hash cookies are renowned for space travel. I can confirm it.

A deep mellowness enfolded me. My mind was tiptoeing through tulips. I said aloud . . . or did I? . . . "I love my life."

That's the best indicator of my condition. Time later, I got the munchies and began to eye the green chicken. Luckily, a frozen pizza had somehow survived my recent campaigns, and I got stuck into that. Halfway through, I fell asleep. Out for six hours. If I dreamt, it was of "Hotel California".

When I came to, my hangover had abated. Not gone but definitely not howling. After a shower and oh so careful shave, I headed for my video shelf. It's sparse but has my very essentials:

Paris, Texas
Once Upon a Time in the West

Sunset Boulevard
Double Indemnity
Cutter's Way
Dog Soldiers

In 1976, Newton Thornberg wrote *Cutter and Bone*. Three ruined survivors of the sixties share a house. Cutter, a crazed crippled Vietnam vet. Bone, a draft dodging dropout. Mo, a mother and agoraphobic alcoholic. They investigate the murder of a young prostitute. They piss off the wrong people, and Mo and her baby are killed.

Cutter and Bone track a capitalist they hold responsible. Cutter, according to Bone,

has a savagery of despair. It precluded his responding to any idea or situation with anything except laughter. His mind was a house of mirrors, distortion reflecting distortion.

Cutter operates on two things:
Despair
Cynicism

Robert Stone wrote *Dog Soldiers* in 1973. Karl Reisz adapted it for the screen in 1978.

Again, it's three fucked people.

Marge, hooked on pharmaceuticals. Her husband, John Converse, a war correspondent, and Hicks, who brings drugs into the States. John Converse sells out his friend to the DA and realises fear was extremely important to him. Morally speaking, it was the basis of his life. I am afraid, therefore I am.

Hicks, pursued by villains and agents, dies in an old hippie cave. Written on the wall is

THERE ARE NO METAPHORS

I watched these movies back to back and felt, as I had felt all my life . . . fuckit.

"One door I passed revealed a man
fully dressed in an antique zoot suit
and a white ten gallon hat.
As I passed by we regarded each other
as two wary lizards might stare as
they slithered across some barren stone."

Walter Mosley, White Butterfly

Eleven in the morning, I'm sitting on a bench at Eyre Square. The debris of Sunday night is mildly stirring. Four o'clock, in the hours before dawn, that's when it's the war zone. The clubs and fast food joints disgorge the hordes.

The fights and yahoo-ism begin.

Top of the square is a statue of Pádraig Ó Conaire. They beheaded him. Christmas two years ago, a yob torched the crib.

Down near the public toilet, a young lad was murdered.

A city on the predatory move.

Progress my arse!

I'd a battered copy of Richard Fariña's *Been Down So Long It Seems Like Up To Me* in my jacket. It's the green faded one. Pockets to burn, like Robert Ginty in *The Exterminator*. Richard Fariña was Joan Baez's brother-in-law. Would probably have written fine books but the dope took him out. I'm running a list in my head:

> Jarrell
> Pavaese
> Plath

Jarrell, from a Caribbean cruiser threw himself and
Gustav Flaubert (1849)

> As my body continues on its
> journey,

            my thoughts keep turning back
            and bury themselves in days past.

Out loud, I mutter, in Irish, *"Och, ochon."*

A New Age traveller approaches, sits on the end of my bench. I'm drinking a cappuccino from a styrofoam.

No chocolate sprinkle. I hate that shit.

The traveller is mid-twenties, bangled in every conceivable area. She says,

"Caffeine will kill you, man."

I don't figure this requires a reply. She says,

"Did you hear me, man?"

"Yeah, so what?"

She scoots a little closer, asks,

"What's with the negative waves?"

A cloud of patchouli envelopes me. I decide to cut through the hippy pose, say,

"Fuck off."

"Oh man, you're transmitting some serious hostility."

My coffee's gone cold and I put it down. She asks,

"Did you have red carpets in your home as a child?"

"What?"

"Feng Shui says it makes a child aggressive."

"We had lino. Brown, puke-tinged shade. It came with the house."

"Oh."

I stand up and she cries,

"Where were you when John died?"

"In bed."

"The Walrus will never die."

"Perish the thought."

And I'm outa there. I look back and she's got the cappuccino on her head, sucking it down.

I'm bursting for a pee and risk the public convenience. A minor drinking school has temporary possession. The place is infamous since a paedophile ring preyed there. The lead wino shouts,

"Want a drink?"

Do I ever, but answer,

"No, but thanks a lot."

My interview with Green Guard is at 12.30 so I still have some time to kill. Catch a glimpse of myself in the mirror, my hair is wild. As I exit, I say,

"Take care."

The school chorus,

"God bless yah, sur."

Off Quay Street, I notice one of the old barber shops. Check my watch, reckon . . . go for it.

There's no customers. A man in his late twenties puts *The Sun* aside, says,

"How you doing?"

"Pretty good, thanks."

I clocked the English accent straight off, asked,

"Didn't this used to be Healy's?"

"You wot?"

He didn't call me "guv" but it hung there, available at a comb's notice. I said,

"I forget the numbers, but I think I want a No. 3."

"You sure?"

"Well, Beckham was a No. 1, so I definitely want up from that."

He motioned to the chair and I sat down. Avoided, to the best of my ability, my own reflection. I asked,

"London?"

"Highbury."

I longed to say, "Highbury and shite talk", opted for "Grand bit of weather."

The music was loud and the guy said,

"Joy Division . . . 1979's 'Unknown Pleasures'."

I kind of liked it. The twisted mix of grace and savagery spoke to my withered sensibility. I said,

"All right."

"Oh yeah, mate, they're the biz. You know, it's twenty years since Ian Curtis drank a bottle of Scotch, watched a Werner Herzog film on TV, turned on a Stooges' album . . ."

He stopped. The punchline was coming and it wasn't going to be good. I could do my role, asked,

"What happened then?"

"He went into the kitchen and hung himself from the clothes rack."

"Christ."

The guy stopped cutting my hair, hung his head. A moment of silence. I asked,

"Why?"

"Dunno. He was caught between a failing marriage and his lover. His health was fucked, and he couldn't get a grip on the band's huge success . . . gel?"

"What do you think?"

"I was you, I'd go for it."

"Bring it on."

He did.

When I was leaving, I gave him a decent tip. He said, "Hey, thanks a lot."

"No, thank you."

I had phoned the security firm early in the morning. Using a false name, I said I wanted a job. Was asked,

"Any experience?"

"I was in the services."

"Great."

I wanted to see if any of their staff recognised me. From there, I was going to have to make it up as I went along. Worst scenario, I might even get a job.

En route, I went into Zhivago Records. The manager, Declan, was one of a rare to rarer species, a Galwegian. He said,

"How's it going?"

"Okay."

"Jeez, what happened to your hair."

"It's a No. 3."

"It's a bloody disgrace. What's stuck in it?"

"That's gel."

"Saw you coming more like."

"I want to buy a record, so could we cut the chit-chat?"

"Testy! What were you looking for?"

"Joy Division."

He laughed out loud.

"You . . . ?"

"Christ, do you want to sell me a record or not?"

"The compilation album . . . that's the one."

"OK."

He knocked a few quid off, so I figured he'd earned the cracks. Outside, I took a deep breath, said, "Showtime."

"Linda put her hand on his arm. 'You know, you don't have to do this.'
He turned to her, a little surprised. 'We want to find out what happens next, don't we?'
'I forgot,' Linda said, 'you're using me. I'm an idea for a movie.'
Chili said, 'We're using each other.'"

Elmore Leonard, *Be Cool*

The security office was on Lower Abbeygate Street. I went in and a receptionist asked me to wait, saying,

"Mr Reynolds will see you in a moment."

I'd barely sat when she called me. The minute I walked in, the man behind the desk did a double take. I glanced at his hands. The knuckles were bruised and cut. We stood staring at each other. I said,

"Surprise!"

He stood up, a big man, all of it muscle, said,

"We don't have any vacancies."

"Too bad. I think I could do 'rent-a-thug'."

"I have no idea what you're talking about."

I held up my bandaged fingers, said,

"Like your work."

He made to move from the desk, and I said,

"I'll see myself out."

The receptionist gave me a shy smile, said,

"Get the job?"

"Got the job done all right."

Outside, I took a deep breath. So, I'd proved a link, but what did that give me? Rang Sutton and told him; he said,

"Well, we're on our way."

"But to where?"

"Hell, I'd say."

"At least it will be familiar."

Back home that evening, I was slow working through a six pack. The doorbell went. Answered to Linda, the bank clerk upstairs tenant. She went,

"Good heavens, what happened to you?"

"Just a scratch."

"Drunk, I suppose."

"Did you want something?"

"I'm having a party tonight, just a few friends."

"You're inviting me?"

"Well yes, but there are some ground rules."

"I'll be there."

And I shut the door. Had just opened a fresh beer when the doorbell went again. Figuring "There goes the party," I pulled the door open. It was Ann Henderson. I said,

"Oh."

"You were expecting someone else."

"No, I mean . . . come in."

She had a batch of shopping bags, said,

"I thought you could use a solid meal. No! I knew you could use a solid meal. But first I need a shot of colada."

"Pina colada?"

She gave me a look of almost contempt, said,

"It's the highest dose of caffeine and sugar in a shot glass."

"Wouldn't a Scotch do the same job?"

Another look.

She found the kitchen. Not a difficult task as there are only two other rooms. I heard her gasp,

"Oh . . . my . . . God!"

"Sorry, I haven't had much time to clean."

"Come in. I'm opening the wine."

I did.

Already she was unpacking bags, sifting through pots, asked,

"Like spaghetti?"

"Shouldn't I?"

"It's dinner."

"Love it."

After she poured the wine, she ordered me out. I sat in the living room, finishing the beer. I didn't really want to put wine down on top but thought, "Fuckit." Which is the short version of the Serenity Prayer.

Half an hour later, we were seated at the table, mountains of food before us. She asked,

"Want to say grace?"

"Can't hurt."

"Thank you, Lord, for this food and drink."

I nodded.

I tried to eat politely. She shook her head, said,

"Jack, there is no way you can look cool and eat spaghetti. Let it dribble, eat like an Italian."

I hate to admit it but I liked her using my name. Throwing caution to the wind, I ate like a demon. She watched me, said,

"I'd forgotten what a pleasure it is to watch a man eat."

Even the wine wasn't half bad. I said,

"Wanna party?"

"I beg your pardon?"

"Upstairs . . . my neighbour . . . she disapproves of me, but I think she'd be surprised by you."

"Why?"

"Well, you're a surprising lady."

She stood up, asked,

"Dessert?"

"No . . . I'm as full as a tick."

I was wearing a grey sweatshirt that read AYLON. The W had long since washed away. I had stone-worn black cords and Du Barry moccasins. I looked like an ad. For GAP retro.

Ann was wearing a red sweatshirt. No logo. Faded blue jeans and pale Reeboks. We could have done one of those mortgage commercials. I didn't mention this. She said,

"We're not really dressed for a party, are we?"

"But we're comfortable, right? They'll think we're an old relaxed couple."

This made her sad. I did what you do in such cases; I said,

"Another drink?"

"Why do you drink so much, Jack?"

I could feel the evening getting away from me. I moved to my bookcase, took a volume out, flicked through, found the well thumbed passage, handed it over, said,

"Will you read this?"

She did.

It's always the same. When you come out of it and take a look around, the sight of wounds that you have left on the people who care for you makes you wince more than those you have inflicted on yourself. Though I am devoid of regret or remorse for almost anything I have done, if there is a corner for these feelings then it lies with that awareness. It should be enough to stop you from ever going back down there, but it seldom is.

Anthony Loyd, *My War Gone By, I Miss It So.*

I went into the bathroom, examined my No. 3. The gel was congealing. I considered a fast shampoo but thought "Screw it." When I came back, Ann had left the book aside, said,

"That is so sad."

"Does it clarify anything?"

"I don't know."

I didn't want to get into this so said,

"Let's get to that party."

"Shouldn't we bring something?"

"Isn't there a bottle of wine left?"

"Oh, right."

We went up the stairs in an awkward silence. At Linda's door, we could hear music. Sounded like James Taylor. Jeez, what a bad omen. Knocked.

Linda answered. She was dressed in a long flowing sheath. I said,

"I brought a friend."

Linda hesitated for just a second, then,

"Lovely. Do come in."

We did.

Everyone was dressed to the nines. The women in long dresses, the guys in suits. We looked like the hired help. Ann went,

"Uh-oh."

I introduced Linda to Ann. They regarded each other with cool assessment. Linda asked,

"What do you do, Ann?"

"I clean offices."

"I see."

But she didn't.

A bar was set up along the wall. Complete with a bartender. He had a waistcoat and bow tie. I took Ann's hand, said to Linda,

"Later."

The barman said,

"Good evening, folks. What can I get you?"

Ann had white wine. I acted as if I were undecided, then,

"Gimme a double tequila."

Ann sighed. I think the barman did too, but it was subdued. He asked,

"Lemon and salt?"

"Naw, skip the crap."

Heavy chunky glass. I was pleased to see the base had one of those super-glued stickers. It read:

Roches

£4.99

A suit approached Ann, began his social skills. I joined as he was saying,

"On Sky News, before I left, they said a man was found crucified in North-West London."

"Oh God!"

The guy let his hand rest lightly on Ann's arm, said,

"Don't worry, the report said his injuries weren't life threatening."

I said, "Hardly life enhancing either."

Linda approached with a tall guy, said,

"Jack, I'd like you to meet Johann, my fiancée."

"Congratulations."

Johann gave me a close look, asked,

"What is your profession, Jackues?"

"That's Jack. I'm unemployed."

Linda gave a tight smile, said,

"Johann is from Rotterdam, he's a programmer."

"Great, my telly's on the blink."

Malice
with a Galway-ed
bite

Ann was on her third glass of wine. Oh yeah, I was counting. Easier then counting my own. I was still on the tequila. John Wayne used to say it hurt his back. Every time he drank it, he fell off his stool.

Linda approached, asked,

"Might I have a word?"

"Fire away."

"A quiet word."

The music had grown in volume. Sounded suspiciously like techno Gary Numan. That awful. Linda led me to the bedroom. Closed the door. I said,

"Alas, I'm spoken for."

She ignored this, sat on the bed. The room was cluttered with furry animals,

> Pink bears
> Pink frogs
> Pink tigers

Leastways, I think that's the colour. I wasn't about to verify. Linda said,

"You'll be aware I've been doing very well at the bank."

"That's good . . . isn't it?"

"Of course. They have generously agreed to help me buy a house."

"Way to go, Linda."

"This house."

"Oh."

"I'll be doing major renovations."

"Ah, don't worry about that. I'm out all day."

"Jack . . . I'm afraid I'll have to ask you to leave."

For a bizarre moment, I thought she meant the bedroom. Then I rallied, tried,

"I'm a sitting tenant."

As opposed to a sitting duck.

Being evicted is no doubt a shock to the system. The mind is liable to turn in any direction. I thought of guns. Well, a gun. I said,

"Did you know Special Garda Units are getting a new pistol. Not just any pistol but the Rolls Royce of handguns."

"I beg your pardon."

"Oh yeah. The Sig Sauer P-226 has been issued to members of the Emergency Response Unit."

"What on earth are you talking about?"

"It's Swiss. That's where the precision comes in. See, all that neutrality gave them time to design a serious weapon. Do you think there's a moral there?"

"Jack . . . I'm serious, you'll have to find new accommodation."

"Course, you being in the bank business, you're not going to piss on the Swiss."

She stood up, said,

"I must get back to the party."

"They're £700 a pop. I don't suppose the lottery will spring for them."

She was at the bedroom door, said,

"Come on, Jack."

"No, I'm going to sit here and think of weapons."

She was gone.

I didn't think I could move into the Skeff with Sutton. Maybe it was time to make that move to London. A knock on the door. I said,

"Yeah."

Ann came in, asked,

"What are you doing, Jack?"

"Talking to pink teddy bears."

"A bad sign."

"Oh yes, but for who . . . *me* or the teds?"

"Linda looked very serious when she came back to the party. What happened?"

"We were discussing guns."

"Guns."

Back at my flat, Ann said,

"I feel a bit tipsy."

"Want to prolong it?"

"Good heavens, no."

There was an awkward silence. I didn't know what to do. She said,

"Will you kiss me?"

I did, if badly. She said,

"That's a poor effort, try again."

I got better.

Then we were in bed and it was wonderful. Slow, strange, exciting. After, she said,

"It's been so long."

"Me too."

"Really?"

"Oh yeah."

Then her voice wavered, she said,

"I haven't mentioned Sarah all evening."

"You don't have to, she's there in your eyes all the time."

She hugged me close, said,

"What a beautiful thing to say."

I felt better than I had in longer than I'd ever admit. Then she asked,

"Did you ever love someone?"

"There was a woman, when I was in the guards. She made me feel more than I was."

"That's a good feeling."

"But I screwed it up."

"Why?"

"It's what I do best."

"That's no answer."

"I could say it was the booze, but that's not true. There's a self-destruct button in me. I keep returning to it."

"You can change."

"I don't know if I want to."

On that sombre note, we went to sleep.

She was gone when I woke. A note on the pillow,

Dear Jack,
You're a lovely man. Don't self-destruct on me.
I couldn't bear it.
                    Xxxxxxxxxxxxxx
                    Ann.

I wasn't sure what I'd let myself in for.

89

A conscience full
of
others' dreams

I never meant to kill him.

A current expression, "It got away from me", is hackneyed beyond tolerance. Used to excuse everything from

>Wife battering
>
>to
>
>Drunk driving

Well, it got away from me. What began as an exercise in *intimidation* ended in murder. Here's how it went down.

After my sojourn with Ann, I met Sutton the next day. Sojourn is a lovely word, has a resonance of culture and wonder. So I was feeling good, feeling strong and ready. I made arrangements for Sutton to pick me up at Seapoint, the huge ballroom that sits sentinel to Salthill.

I'd served my dancing apprenticeship to the late sixties showbands there.

What bands!

>Brendan Bowyer
>
>The Indians
>
>The Freshmen

Those guys came on stage at nine, played non-stop for hours. And did they give it large. Flogged their guts out with cover versions of everything from

>"Suspicious Minds"
>
>to
>
>"If I didn't have a dime . . ."

If not a time of innocence, it was most definitely an era of enthusiasm.

As I sat on the promenade, The Specials' "Ghost Town" was playing in my head. A No. 1 from 1981, it caught perfectly the civic unrest of London back then.

Sutton pulled up in a Volvo. It looked seriously battered. I got in and asked,

"Where did you find this?"

It was an automatic and he set it on cruise, said,

"Bought it from a Swede in Clifden."

He glanced at me, asked,

"What's the difference with you?"

"Me?"

"Yeah, you've got a shit-eating grin going there."

"Do I?"

"Yeah, like the cat got the cream."

Then he slapped the wheel with his palm, exclaimed,

"I get it . . . you got laid . . . you dirty dog, you did, didn't you?"

"I got lucky."

"Well I never! Good ol' Taylor. Who was it, that rock chick, what's her face, Cathy B.?"

"Nope."

"Don't make me do the hundred guesses trip. Or did you get a hooker, eh?"

"Ann Henderson."

"The dead girl's mother?"

"Yeah."

"Jeez, Taylor, how bright was that?"

Cathy B. had found Ford's address. When I'd told Sutton, he asked,

"The guy isn't married?"

"No."

"Let's go visit his gaff, see what shakes."

We parked at the side of Blackrock. The Salthill Towers loomed behind us. Sutton asked,

"Where's he located?"

"Ground floor."

Breaking in was a breeze. The lock was one of those Yale jobs. We walked into a spacious living room, expensively furnished. Tidy, too. A long coffee table had a book, openended, but nothing else. I checked the title, *Finnegans Wake*. Sutton said,

"Yeah, like anyone actually reads this."

We did a thorough search, found nothing. Sutton asked,

"You sure anybody lives here?"

"There's suits in the wardrobe, food in the fridge."

Sutton leaned against the sitting room wall, said,

"See this carpet?"

"Expensive, I'd say."

"But it's not level. See near the lamp, it rises slightly."

"So?"

"So, let's roll that sucker."

With the carpet back, we stared at loose floorboards. Sutton bent down, pushed them aside, said,

"Bingo."

Began to hand up a series of videos. A batch of magazines, too. A glance showed the subject, child pornography. Sutton said,

"Put all this crap on the table."

I did.

We checked out two of the videos. More of the same. Sutton asked,

"What now?"

"Let's wait for him."

We raided the fridge, found some nice steaks, got them cooking. Round 6.30, I was dozing when I heard a key in the lock. Sutton was standing, looking relaxed. Ford came in, was into the sitting room before he saw us. Sutton had moved to the door. Ford glanced at the table, its piled contents. If he was panicked, he hid it well; he asked,

"What do you want?"

"Information."

"Ah."

"Tell me about Sarah Henderson, the other girls."

He sat down, looked towards Sutton, said,

"More ex-garda."

"Does it matter?"

"No, I suppose not."

"So Mr Ford, tell all."

"It's no big deal. Mr Planter likes young girls. Sometimes they get awkward, start making threats.

94

What can I say, they get depressed, go for the long swim."

Till then, I'd stayed calm. But something in his smug expression, the contempt in his voice, got me. I was up and smacking him across the face. I pulled him to his feet and he spat at me. I threw him from me, and his head came down heavily on the coffee table. He didn't move. Sutton was over, checking for a pulse, said,

"The fucker's gone."

"What?"

"He's dead."

"Christ."

"We better get out of here. We clean off everything."

We even put the videos back in place. As we left, Sutton wiped the door handle, said,

"Let's hope they think he fell."

A
GRIM
ARTICULATION

Sutton dropped me off at my home. We hadn't spoken on the way. He asked now,

"Do you want me to come in?"

"No."

"You going to be OK?"

"I've no idea."

"Look, Jack . . . listen. It was an accident. Plus, how big a loss is he? The guy was garbage, the world is better off without him."

"Yeah, I'll see you."

I'd just opened the front door when Linda appeared. She said,

"Ah, Jack."

I didn't answer, brushed past her. Heard her exclaim,

"Well, I never!"

Like I gave a rat's ass. First off, I had a shower, scrubbed my skin till it hurt. Could feel Ford's spittle on my face, like a burn. The phone rang. I growled,

"What?"

"Jack, it's Ann."

"Yeah . . . what?"

"Are you all right?"

"Christsake. I wish people would stop asking that."

I slammed the phone down. Put on an XL sweatshirt with the logo:

KNICKS KICK ASS

A pair of ultra-faded 501s. One more wash and they were history. Usually, I put this gear on, I chill.

Wasn't happening.

Got out a bottle of brandy. I'm a philistine, I hate cognac. The hangovers are total slaughter. Cracked the seal. Into the kitchen and washed *the* glass. The Roches £4.99 was still visible on the base. Rinsed it twice to erase the tequila scent. Back to the sitting room. The steak I'd eaten at Ford's place sat in my gut like a lump of lead.

I tried to recall all my resolution about the brandy. Especially how J.M. O'Neill said it takes away the very air it gave you.

Aloud I said,

"Yeah, yeah . . . yada yada," and sank the first one.

OK.

Not so bad. In fact, if it erred, it was on the smooth side.

Poured another.

In AA they warn about self-pity. "Poor me, poor me, pour me another." Well, I was already drinking.

Right!

Certainly, pity was the very last thing I was feeling.

Pity the poor fuck who walloped his head offa the coffee table. Or was that — had his head walloped against it? I tried to shut out that image.

What loss was he? A pervert who preyed on young girls.

This wouldn't fly, I couldn't fan a single flame of justification.

The phone went. Picked it up, tried,

"Yeah?"

"Jack, it's Sutton."

"Oh, yeah."

"How you doing there?"

"I'm OK."

"Drinking, huh?"

"What?"

"I can hear it in your speech."

"What are you? My mother?"

"Hey, drop the tone. I just want to say you're not alone, buddy. I'll swing by, we can order up a storm of pizza, catch a vid."

"Like a date."

"Jesus, Jack. Whatever you're drinking, it's not agreeing with you."

"Neither are you."

And I hung up.

Now I was up, pacing, talking.

"Who needs you, the fuck I do. And people stop calling me."

I tore the phone line out.

Turned the radio on, hit Lyric by mistake. Were playing "Fur Elise". I thought, I love that and first thing tomorrow, I'm going out to buy it. Time later, after chasing the dial and hitting four other stations, I was also going to buy:

> Elvis
> The Eagles
> James Last
> and
> The Furey Bros.

Then thought, "Why wait?"

Glanced at the cognac. Oh-my-God! Nearly empty. Did I spill some? Yeah, must have, that would explain it. Took some organisation to get ready as I bumped into furniture, but finally I was set, shouted,

"Sayonara, suckers."

The empty room didn't answer.

"Doctor, I'm in trouble."
"Oh,
goodness, gracious me"

Sophia Loren and Peter Sellers, *The Millionairess*

Came to with restraints on my wrists. The mother of a hangover. I was strapped down on what appeared to be a trolley. My head was pounding. Tremors were running up my legs. I had no recollection of anything after "Sayonara, suckers."

A nurse appeared, said,

"Ah, Mr Taylor, I'll get the doctor."

She did.

A man in his fifties, a vague smile, leaned over me, said,

"Mr Taylor, I'm Dr Lee. Do you remember how you got here?"

Tried to shake my head but the pain was too fierce. He nodded, said,

"You're in Ballinasloe . . . the mental hospital. My guess is you were operating in a blackout. You collapsed outside Hayden's Hotel."

Terror was assaulting every fibre. Sweat cascaded down my body. The doctor said,

"We had to reset your fingers as it appears you punched somebody. Not a good idea with fingers recently broken."

I managed to get some saliva going, asked,

"What about my nose?"

He laughed out loud, said,

"No, we had to admit defeat on that front. But I'm glad you've kept your sense of humour. You're going to need it."

The nurse gave me a shot and I was gone again. If there were dreams, thank Christ they're beyond recall. When next I surfaced, I felt a little less awful. The restraints were gone, so something was changing if not improving. Dr Lee again.

"Do you remember our talk?"

"I do."

"That was forty-eight hours ago."

I tried to look suitably awed, but in a mental hospital, what's awe? He continued,

"You're making a rapid recovery. The body is an amazing thing. Despite ferocious punishment, it battles to regroup. But for what, Mr Taylor?"

I was finally able to speak without gasping for saliva. I said,

"I don't understand the question."

"Oh, I think you do, Mr Taylor. Why should we fix you up so you can go right out and do the exact same thing again?"

I had no idea.

"I've no idea."

"You've been down this road before."

"I have. Could you call me Jack?"

"Jack! Well, Jack, I could try and frighten you with horror stories. Every time you blackout, it's a rehearsal for a wet brain. Your liver is in bad shape, and I don't know how much more your kidneys can endure. Any questions?"

I wanted to know why on earth I'd come to Ballinasloe, but didn't think he could answer that. I said,

"Thanks . . . for . . . well . . . not reading me the riot act."

"I thought I just did."

After my initial days of drying out, I was given my clothes. They'd been cleaned and pressed. My delight at having them was huge. Stood in the middle of the room, did a little jig. Shaky . . . and brief, but definitely a few steps of Irish near-abandon.

It's a sad fact that a fully grown man should be so grateful just to be dressed.

I was released into general population. Asked the nurse,

"Couldn't I stay in my room?"

Big laugh and,

"What do you think this is . . . a hotel? Get out and circulate."

I didn't know what to expect. A mental hospital . . . wouldn't psychos be roaming freely. In every sense of the word, I anticipated bedlam. Drooling patients, straitjackets, derangement on foot.

What I got was quiet. Not silence but a muted burr. As if the volume had been turned way down. The wonders of medication. Keep them doped, you keep them docile.

Lunch was being served in the refectory. A bright open room, not unlike our canteen at training in Templemore.

I took a tray and joined the queue. The line was orderly and . . . quiet. A voice behind me said,

"First time?"

Turned to face a man in his late sixties. He didn't look . . . mad! Well dressed with a porter face. The nose a scarlet mess of burst vessels. His build had once been impressive but had collapsed badly. I said,

"Does it show?"

"You're jumping out of your skin."

"Oh."

He put out his hand, hands like Larry Cunningham. Big craw thumpers. We shook. His grip was surprisingly gentle. He said,

"I'm Bill Arden."

"Jack Taylor."

"Hello, Jack Taylor."

I'd reached the hot food section. The server, a fat country woman, asked,

"What can I get you, love?"

The "love" walloped my heart. I wanted to hug her. Bill said,

"The bacon and cabbage is lovely."

I ordered that. She said,

"Gravy, love?"

"Please."

Dessert was stewed apple and custard. Lashings of it. I took that too. What the hell. I wasn't intending to eat anyway. Bill said,

"Grab a spot near the window. I'll bring tea."

I did.

The people at the table were chowing down. Eating as if their lives depended on it. Maybe they did.

Bill sat, immediately dug into the food. Ate like a horse. Mid-chew, he looked up, asked,

"You're not eating?"

"No."

"They take notice . . . better play the game."

Pieces of cabbage had lodged in his front teeth. I couldn't tear my eyes from them. I moved my fork listlessly through my own heap. Bill said,

"Slide it down the table, let the monkeys help."

I did. The contents were demolished in seconds flat, the empty plate slid back. Bill said,

"I'll have your dessert, I'm a sucker for sweet things."

Finally finished, he sat back, loosened the top button of his pants and belched. Pulled out a pack of cigarettes, asked,

"Smoke?"

"No . . . thanks."

He fired up, blew a cloud of smoke, said,

"Stick around, you will."

"Doubt it."

Then I noticed everybody — and I mean *everybody* — was smoking. Even the biddy behind the food counter was having a puff. He caught my look, said,

"A man having a share of the market would be set for life."

I wasn't sure where to go with that so I said,

"It's a thought."

Even as I felt, it was a shitty thought. Bill asked,

"You're alky?"

"Come again?"

"An alcoholic, that's why you're here . . . right?"

Decided it was as good a time as any other to wax American, said,

"I guess."

"I knew it. Can always spot the boozers. We have our own antennae. So, you doing the Unit?"

"The what?"

"Alcoholic Unit — the one here is the best in the country. I've done it many times."

"No offence, Bill, but if it's so hot, how come you're here . . . again?"

"I tell you, Jack, I love to drink. When I go on a tear, I give them a ring, tell them to hold a bed. Two, shit . . . three times a year, I'm in."

"Christ!"

"Don't knock it till you've tried it. You're out there causing mayhem, it's a comfort to know you have a haven."

A shudder passed through me. He looked at me. I said,

"Withdrawal."

"Get another blast of the Librium, fix you right up."

A man was passing, lurched into me, straightened, then weaved from side to side to the door. Bill grinned, said,

"That's the Ballinasloe special."

"What is?"

"Yer man, watch . . . see him sway . . . as if he was pissed. It's the Largactil shuffle. Swoon to your own drummer, in orbit all the day long. Jesus, I love this place."

I was getting a little bit tired of Bill. All that midlands bonhomie is very wearing. He said,

"Any questions?"

"Um . . ."

"I'm yer man. There's nothing happens I don't know about . . . or a way around."

And, to my absolute horror, he fucking winked. If I live to be a hundred, doubtful though that be, I'll never forget it. Stands as one of those moments of pure unadulterated awfulness. Fighting to keep my face in neutral, I said,

"There is one thing."

"Whatever, I live to serve."

"Where's the library?"

He appeared profoundly shocked, took a minute then said,

"You're kidding me."

"Listen, *Bert* . . ."

"It's Bill!"

"Whatever. I realise you've known me all of ten minutes, but ask yourself, in all seriousness . . . do I look like a kidder?"

"No."

"So . . . the library?"

He was confused, wanted to hit back, said,

"You sure don't look like a reader."

My turn to laugh. If you don't laugh at least once in the asylum, time to up the medicine. I asked,

"What does a reader look like?"

"Jesus, I don't know, a serious bastard . . . a . . ."

"Bill . . . yo, Bill, take this on trust . . . I'm one serious guy."

He wasn't throwing in the towel yet. No wonder them midland crowd make good farmers. He rushed,

"But you're a boozer, you admitted it. When do you get time to read?"

"Between bouts. When I'm laid up, I read."

"I never heard the banging of that. Between skites I'm in bed . . . dying."

"I've always been a reader; no matter what else I lost, I hung on to that."

He lit another cigarette, grunted,

"They don't like you reading."

"Gee, that's going to weigh on my conscience. So, Bill, where is it?"

"On the first floor. You won't be able to go, it's OT after dinner."

"O what?"

"Occupational therapy, making baskets."

It had finally come to pass. I stood on the precipice of being a basket case. The nurses began to wheel round the medication trolley. Got my jolt of Librium and said to Bill,

"Catch you later."

"But it's OT!"

A whinge had crept into his voice. I stood up, said,

"Books are my therapy."

I heard Bill mutter,

"Divil a queerer sort of alky I ever met."

BOOKS AND ALL POINTS WEST

There's always been books. All my bedraggled life, they've been the only constant. Even Sutton, my closest friend, had exclaimed,

"What's with the fucking reading, man? You used to be a guard, for christsakes."

Which is Irish logic at its finest.

I'd said to him then and umpteen times since,

"Reading transports me."

He said with his characteristic candour,

"Shite talk."

As I've said, my father worked on the railways. He loved cowboy books. There was always a battered Zane Grey in his jacket. He began to pass them on to me. My mother would say,

"You'll make a sissy out of him."

When she wasn't within earshot, he'd whisper,

"Don't mind your mother. *She means well.* But you keep reading."

"Why, Dad?"

Not that I was going to stop, I was already hooked.

"They'll give you options."

"What's options?"

A faraway look would come into his eyes and then,

"Freedom, son."

For my tenth birthday, he gave me a library card. My mother gave me a hurley. She was frequently to use the same stick to wallop the bejaysus outa me. I did play hurling. How else could I have qualified for the Garda Síochána? No one appreciates a good hurler more.

The library card was a "ticket to ride". In those days the library was located in the Court House. Books above, courts below. Each time I went, I gazed at the gardaí in awe. Then upstairs to gaze at the books in wonder. The two threads of my life had been interwoven.

One literally led to the other. I have been unable to shed the influence of both no matter what the circumstances of my life have been.

I began with Robert Louis Stevenson, Richmal Crompton, the Hardy Boys. No doubt I'd have continued in a haphazard fashion, eventually losing interest, if not for head librarian at the time, Tommy Kennedy. A tall thin man with an air of other-worldliness. My first few visits, he'd glance at my selection, go "mmm . . ." and stamp them.

One particularly wet dark Tuesday, he'd approached me, said,

"I think it's time we organised your reading."

"Why?"

"Do you want to get bored?"

"No."

Started me out with Dickens. Gradually eased me into the classics without any fanfare. Always, he kept it at low key, let me believe it was my choice.

Later, when teenage tornadoes played havoc with everything, he introduced crime fiction. Kept me reading.

He also put books aside, then later I'd get a parcel containing

> poetry
> philosophy
> and the hook
> American crime novels.

I'd now become a bibliophile in the true sense of the word. Not only did I love to read, I loved the actual books. Had learnt to appreciate the smell, the binding, the print, the actual feel of the volumes.

My father had built me a large bookcase, and I'd learnt to line the books alphabetically and according to category.

I was also running wild. Playing hurling, drinking cider, barely attending school. But back home, I'd gaze at my library with a glow in my heart.

Because I loved the look and feel of a volume, I'd begin to read it. That's how I started to find poetry. I was never to find it in my life, but it was always within reach.

Not a fucking word of this was I saying to another human being. Mention poetry in our street and you'd lose your balls.

My father frequently stood in front of the growing collection, would say,

"Kenny's themselves would be proud of it."

My mother, disgusted, had her party piece.

"Filling his head with mad notions. I'd like to try telling the rent man he can have some poems."

My father would give me a look and I'd mouth silently,

113

"*She means well.*"

Later, I'd lie in bed, hear her rant,

"And I suppose you'll tell me we can eat books. I'd like to see them buy a loaf of bread."

In fact, she did get her wish. My first day away at Templemore, she sold them and used the bookcase for the fire.

Tommy Kennedy had forecast great things for me. Dreamed I'd even go to college. My exam results barely got me accepted as a guard. When I told Tommy my career choice, he put his head in his hands, said,

"What a crying shame."

The night before I left, I met him in Garavan's. I was big then, hurling and potatoes adding bulk and muscle. I was in Garavan's waiting. Tommy came in, squinted through the half light. I shouted,

"Mr Kennedy."

Life had worn him down. He had the shape of an old greyhound. An air of melancholy in his wake. I asked,

"What will it be, Mr Kennedy?"

"A bottle of stout."

Ablaze with youth and bravado, I got the drinks. Pint for me. Tommy said,

"You're starting early."

I looked at my new watch, shining on its plastic strap. A Woolworths' special. He gave a sad smile, said,

"I didn't mean that."

I said,

"*Slainte.*"

"Good luck, Jack."

114

We fell to silence. Then he produced a slim volume, said,

"A going-away gift."

Beautifully bound, old leather cover, gilt edging. He said,

"It's Francis Thompson, *The Hound of Heaven*. I hope it never gains significance for you."

I had nothing for him. He said,

"I could still send you the parcels."

"Um . . . better not . . . you know . . . country fellahs, they'd think I was queer."

He stood up then, shook my hand. I said,

"I'll write."

"Do that. God bless."

Course I never did . . . write, that is. To my eternal shame, he was dead two years before I heard.

SUTTON

My time in Ballinasloe, I thought of a hundred things. Most of a depressive nature. The roads not less travelled but blindly staggered upon. People who'd been kind to me and I had abused so very badly.

A reckless disregard for the feelings of others. Oh yeah. I had a shitload of guilt. Add a dash of remorse and gallons of self-pity, you had the classic alcoholic in all his tarnished glory.

Outside, I dealt with this baggage through drink. Just blot those suckers way on out. Numb the pain. The paradox being that each fresh numbness trailed fresh damage in its wake.

Behold a pale rider, tanked to the gills.

The first few hospital days, the time of detox, you were encouraged to drink lots of water. Flush those toxins away. I could do that. You had a blood test to calculate the damage to kidneys and liver. Mine had taken a fine hammering. Daily shots of multivitamins to drag the system screaming back to health. Librium of course. Then my favourite, a sleeper for those nights. The night holding the most terror for the alky.

Did I dream? You betcha. But not any of the predictables. Not

> my dead father
> dead friends
> dead life

No.

I dreamt of Sutton.

Our friendship had been instant. One of those inexplicable bondings that defy analysis. I was a young guard, green as cabbage in most things. He was then a grizzled barman, veteran of numerous skirmishes, real and imaginary. Even now, I'm unsure of his nationality, his age, his background.

They changed as often as the pubs we prowled. Over numerous sessions, he told me he'd been, variously

A soldier

entrepreneur

painter

criminal

There was a kernel of truth in each telling, but the details shifted and swayed so often you could never nail down one particular fact.

He was your true chameleon. Blending into whatever surrounding he'd then selected. When I met him, he'd a full-blown northern accent. Could sound like Ian Paisley as easily as Eamonn McCann.

Now that's impressive, not to mention frightening.

I once heard him mimic Bernadette Devlin to an eerie degree.

When he moved to Galway, he'd the accent down in a week. You'd swear he'd never been past Tuam.

None of this set off any warning bells to me. I believed it made him fascinating.

Because I was essentially deaf, to the important things, because I was young . . .

118

because
because
because

Because maybe I didn't want to acknowledge his darkness, I let a whole series of signposts slide by me.

From the off, he'd been upfront about the violence. Had told me of bar fights when he'd near murdered his opponents, adding,

"Know what, Jack?"

"Yeah?"

"I regret it."

"Well, it sometimes gets out of hand."

"Fuck, no, I don't mean that. I regret I didn't kill the bastards."

I laughed it off.

My time off was erratic. As the "troubles" flared, ignited, I could pull duty for forty-eight hours at a stretch. But no matter when my breaks came, Sutton would stop work, and off we'd roar on the batter.

One memorable Saturday night/Sunday morning, we'd drunk long and hard in a shebeen on the Lower Falls. The palpable air of danger and gunsmoke only heightened the rush. I swear you could taste cordite in the pints. Sutton's face was glowing; he said,

"Man, this is it, the absolute best it gets."

From that trip, I still have a hand-carved two foot harp. Made by the inmates of Long Kesh. I must have heard "The Men Behind The Wire" a hundred times.

Washing down creamy pints with golden shots of Bushmills, Sutton leant over to me, perspiration rolling off his face, said,

"Isn't this *it*, Jack?"

"It's hopping all right."

"You know what would be the trip?"

"Tell me."

"To kill some bastard."

"What!"

"Yeah . . . just to waste some cunt."

"What?"

He pulled back, pinched me on the shoulder, said, "Only messing . . . you need to lighten up, Jack."

Such moments had happened over the years. I'd swept them under the carpet of empty bottles and monumental hangovers.

Odd times, I got the uneasy feeling he hated me. Could never nail it down and dismissed it as the product of the drink paranoia.

One evening, I was waiting for him at a pub in Newry. I usually had a book hidden on my person, snatching a read at opportune moments. I was thus engrossed when I heard,

"Jesus, Taylor, always with the books."

I moved to put it away, but he grabbed it, read the title, *The Hound of Heaven* said,

"Francis Thompson, eh?"

"You know it?"

He put back his head, recited,

"I fled him down the nights and down the days . . ."

I nodded and he said,

"He died roaring."

"What?"

"It's how alkies go, they die roaring."

"Jesus."

Whenever misgivings arose, I shut them down. Drilled into my mind — "He's my friend. Anyway, who's perfect?"

The library in Ballinasloe was closed. For renovations. My days were spent in OT. A basket of tiny springs on the table. My job, to fit them into biros.

Rest of the time, I gulped Librium, tried to avoid Bill and longed for the sleepers come night.

The last Ballinasloe dream was so vivid, I'm not sure it didn't happen. Sutton saying,

"You're the reader . . . the crime expert in fact."

"Yeah."

"Read Jim Thompson's *The Killer Inside*?"

"Missed that."

"You missed the best one."

But there's a God. And not only in Tom Jones' song. The day of my release, I was given my clothes, fresh washed and ironed. Plus a bulging wallet. No drinker ever ends up with money. It's against the laws of nature. When I'd left my flat, I couldn't have had more than thirty odd quid. I stared at the wallet. The nurse, misreading it, said,

"It's all there, Mr Taylor, we don't steal from our patients. Four hundred and fifty pounds. Count it if you like."

She stormed off. I went to say goodbye to Dr Lee. I said,

"Could I make a contribution?"

"Don't drink."

"I meant . . ."

"So did I."

He put out his hand, said,

"There's AA."

"There is."

"And Antabuse."

"Right."

He didn't shake his head, but the implication was there. Then, he asked,

"Jack . . . have you family . . . friends?"

"Good question."

"Well, you better go find out."

Outside, the sun was shining. A coach paused and every one on the crowded thing stared at me. Backlit by the most infamous asylum in Ireland, with my body in bits, I sure as hell wasn't staff.

I gave them the finger.

Most applauded.

Naturally, but a spit from the hospital was a pub. For one dizzy moment, I was poised. Oh, never did the siren song cry so awful bright. I couldn't . . . I couldn't. I looked back and felt Dr Lee nodded, as if he could see, and I walked on.

At the train station, I'd only half an hour till the train. Sat in the buffet, ordered nothing. There was a newspaper on the chair. More tribunals. I felt I'd gotten my own brown envelope. Checked the date and my stomach did a flip over. I'd been gone for twelve days. One for each of the apostles. Doing some calculating, I'd been three days missing in action and . . . earning money.

The train came and I got a window seat. I hadn't shaved in hospital and a half decent beard was coming in. I looked like Kris Kristofferson's dad. The mangled nose gave a total "don't fuck" look. Leaving the hospital, I'd taken a hard stare in the mirror. Solved what was puzzling me. My eyes. They were clear and nearly alive. Not bright but in the neighbourhood. After years of sickness lodged therein, it was some revelation.

Outside Athenry, the refreshments trolley came. A young lad of eighteen or so asked,

"Tea, coffee, minerals?"

"A tea, please."

I could feel him inspecting my injuries, I said,

"Came off my bike."

"Wow."

"Yeah, doing ninety."

"A Harley?"

"Is there another?"

He loved that, then,

"Do you want a drink?"

"What?"

"Look, see we've all these miniatures, but like, who's gonna pay these prices?"

"No . . . thank you."

"I'll give you two for one. How would that be?"

"I can't . . . I mean . . . I'm on tablets . . . for the pain."

"Ah . . . tablets."

He seemed to know all about them, then,

"I gotta go. You take care."

Alighting from the train, I met a taxi driver I'd known all my life. He said,

"Travelling light!"

"The luggage arrives with the car."

"Wise move."

If you can do this sort of stuff with a straight face, you're elected. Taxi drivers, of course, have to take an exam in it.

I looked out across Eyre Square and pubs beaconed from every corner. Backpackers thronged to and fro in search of Nirvana, a cheap hostel. A drinking school was in full song across from the Great Southern. As there was no one else to say it, I said,

"Welcome home."

THE
DEAD

Walking into Grogan's, I felt a mix of dread and adrenalin. Sean, behind the counter, didn't recognise me. I said,

"Sean."

"Jesus, Mary and Joseph, it's Grizzly Adams."

He came out from behind the counter, said,

"My God, where have you been? The whole country's looking for you. Sit down, sit down, I'll get your usual."

"Sean, no booze . . . just coffee."

"Are you serious?"

"Alas."

"Good man."

You know you're bad when a publican's glad you're not drinking. I sat down, feeling light-headed. Sean came back with the coffee, saying,

"I've given you a Club Milk to take the bare look off it."

I tasted the coffee, said,

"Jeez, tastes good."

He clapped his hands like an excited child, said,

"That's real coffee. Usually I give you any oul dregs, but now . . ."

"It's great, terrific bite."

He laid his hand on my arm, said,

"Tell all."

128

Nothing stops talk like this request. The mind instantly downs tools. But he continued,

"Ann, that woman? She's been in every day, phones all the time . . . and Sutton, he has me damned. Why didn't you phone?"

"I couldn't."

"Oh, I see."

But he didn't. He stood up, said,

"All in good time. I'm delighted you're all right."

After a bit, I decided to try and find Sutton. Which wasn't difficult. He was propping the bar in the Skeff. He didn't bat an eyelid, asked,

"What kept you?"

"I got sidetracked."

"I like the beard, makes you look even meaner. A pint or a short?"

"A Coke."

"A Coke it is. Barman!"

Sutton got a fresh pint and carried it and the Coke to a window table. We sat and he clinked the pint against the Coke, said,

"Cheers."

"Cheers."

"So, was it Ballinasloe?"

"Yeah."

"Dr Lee still there."

"He sure is."

"Decent man."

"I liked him."

Sutton held his pint up to the light, examining it closely, said,

"Did two field trips myself. First time out, I drank right off."

"In that first pub?"

He laughed but without humour, said,

"Yeah, the barstaff there have some attitude, I tell you. Veterans of constant incoming. One of the few places I've been where the bullshit doesn't fly. The hospital send out a mop-up squad come closing. You're there, you're nabbed."

He drained half the pint, continued,

"Second time to bat, I got two days. Was leaping outa my skin. Boy, did I hit the bar with thunder."

"And now?"

"What you see is part of what you got. I drink with the brakes on."

"Does it work?"

"Fuck, no."

I went to order him a fresh pint, kept my eyes down. The barman asked,

"Another Coke?"

"I'd rather slash my wrist."

The barman got a big kick outa this. Back with Sutton, I told him about my loaded wallet. He said,

"You star-trekked about twelve days ago . . . right? I vaguely remember some dope dealer got taken down."

"What?"

"Yeah, some punk kid. At the Salmon Weir Bridge, he got the shite hammered out of him, his earnings lifted. The guards were delighted."

He glanced at my newly bandaged hand, went,

"Mm . . . m . . . hmph."

Then he looked right at me, said,

"How come you haven't asked about Mr Ford, the late lamented paedophile?"

"I hoped it was part of the jigs."

"No worries, pal. Verdict, accidental death. I went to the funeral."

"You're kiddin'."

"Poor attendance. You'd get a bigger crowd for a Hib's game."

I didn't know what to think. Sutton patted my shoulder, said,

"Good fuckin' riddance."

I got home near eight. My flat was cold and forlorn. The empty cognac bottle was by the window. I put the phone back on and rang Ann. She recognised me straightaway, exclaimed,

"Oh, thank God, oh Jack . . . are you okay?"

"Yeah, I'm fine . . . I had to get away . . . I needed some time . . ."

"But you're back now."

"I am."

"That's wonderful. I lit candles for you."

"God knows I needed them."

She laughed then and the tension was broken. I arranged to meet her for lunch next day. After I put the phone down, I wondered why I hadn't said I was sober. Not sober but not drinking. The gulf of difference. If sobriety is "of sound mind" then I had a ways to go. I hadn't said anything to her 'cause I didn't know if I'd be drinking when I met her.

The Coke had given me a splitting headache, but I could hack that. A sense of dis-ease was harder to handle.

I watched some bad television and at eleven turned it off.

In bed, I tossed and turned, but for the life of me, I couldn't recall the face of the paedophile.

ROCK
ME
GENTLY

Is there a soundtrack to dreaming? Like, with nightmares, you get heavy metal or Boyzone. As I slept, it seemed like the mellowest of Southern California were playing. I dreamt of my father. As a very young child, I was holding his hand at Eyre Square. A bus passed and I suddenly realised I could spell . . . I read aloud the ad. On the side . . .

PADDY

He was delighted. Not only because it was the first word I spelt but it was his name. A more cynical view is my first word happened to be *the* Irish whiskey.

But nothing dims the warmth of that moment. I felt completely joined with him. Years, experience, life dented the union so many times, but only superficially.

The phone dragged me up. I couldn't see the time, mumbled,

"Hello."

"Jack, it's Sutton."

"What time is it?"

"Later than we think."

"Jeez, Sutton, what is it?"

"I thought you might be suffering, needing a hit."

"I was sleeping."

134

"Yeah, like I believe that. Anyway, while you were away, some kids took to burning winos."

"What!"

"Yeah, and winos, they're our brothers under the skin. They're walking point. Anyway, I'm here with a few like-minded people, and we're going to nab the kids' ringleader."

"To do what?"

"Burn the fucker."

"Jeez, Sutton."

"So, wanna come along, play with fire?"

"Are you nuts, that's vigilantism."

"It's justice, man."

"Sutton, tell me this. Is this you with or without the brakes on?"

He gave a wild laugh, said,

"Got to go, time to fry."

No return to sleep after that. I paced the floor for a few hours, thought of chewing the wallpaper. Went to the bookcase, selected John Sanford. He'd written twelve in the *Prey* series and I chanced on this.

Coming down hard. He'd been flying on cocaine for three days. Then, last night coming down, he'd stopped at a liquor store for a bottle of Stolichnaya. There was no smooth landing after a three day toot but the vodka turned a wheels-up-belly-landing into a full crash and burn. Now he'd pay. Now he was just gonna have to suck it up.

Enough.

The madness is I then wanted a drink beyond urgency. Not just any drink. Oh no, it would have to be an ice-cold Stoli.

Back to bed. Sleep gave grudgingly and with conditions. I got the nine o'clock news the next morning. Third item in,

A youth was seriously injured after being set on fire in the early hours of the morning. The incident took place on Eyre Square. Gardaí are anxious to trace four men in connection with the attack. Superintendent Clancy, referring to a suggestion that this was in retaliation for recent fire attacks on homeless men, said:

"Any type of vigilantism or private individuals attempting to enforce the law will be vigorously opposed."

He then went rambling on in a mini-state-of-the-nation spiel, but I cut him off.

I was in Grogan's after eleven, and Sean asked anxiously,

"Real coffee or dregs?"

"The best you've got."

It was sad to see how relieved he was to hear that. He returned with a coffee pot and toast, said,

"You'll need a bit o' lining."

I said,

"Sit down, I want to ask you something."

"Fire away."

"Bear in mind the person who's asking you has recently been under . . . shall we say . . . restraints."

He nodded.

"Is it just me or does Sutton seem to have lost it?"

He gave a snort of disgust, said,

"Couldn't never stand him."

"Right . . . but what do you think?"

"I never understood what you saw in him."

This was like pulling teeth.

"Sean . . . Sean, OK . . . I got that, but what do you think?"

"He needs locking up."

"Thanks, Sean. An unbiased opinion was more than I could have dreamed of."

Sean was standing now, spluttering,

"I'll tell you another thing, Jack . . ."

As if I could stop him.

"That fellow's going straight to hell, and he'll bring as many as he can with him."

The said fellow arrived an hour later, said,

"Thought I'd find you here. Sean . . . a pint before Lent."

He examined me close, said,

"Still sober? I'm impressed. You have . . . what, a day?"

"Thirteen days."

"Confinement doesn't count."

"Jesus, it does to me."

Sean brought the drink, plonked it down. Sutton said,

"Cranky oul fucker."

I said,

"I heard the news."

"Gave a great bit of heat . . . for such a small bastard. The best part though, you'll love this, was his mates crying and shouting, 'Call the guards.' Isn't that priceless?"

"You could have killed him."

"Well, we gave it our best shot."

Sutton was beyond wired. As if he'd finally found his calling. He seemed on the verge of giggles. Now he leant close, said,

"It's all down to you, Jack."

"Me!"

"You paved the way with that pervert. Not only are they accountable, they're terminal."

"Come on, Sutton, can't you see, it's madness?"

"Oh, that it is. Glorious lunacy."

138

THE HAND THAT ROCKS THE CRADLE

I'd arranged to meet Ann at the Chinese restaurant. I'd left Sutton mumbling to himself. Sean caught me at the door, said,

"I'm taking down his painting."

"Ah, don't do that, Sean."

"He's hopeless, people want the hurleys back."

"Sean, leave it for a little while, he's a bit fragile at the moment."

"Fragile! That chancer? He'd build a nest in your ear and charge you rent."

I went into Madden's and bought six red roses. I have never, never bought flowers in my life. The assistant said,

"Will I make them into a spray or a bouquet?"

"I dunno."

She laughed, so I said,

"Is there any way you can wrap so . . ."

"So people won't see, is that it?"

"It is."

"Arrah, go on our that. It takes a real man to carry flowers."

"I'm going to have to take your word for it."

No matter how I held them, they were blatant. Of course, that's the day you meet everyone you've ever known. All of them comedians:

"Aw, isn't that sweet."

"Say it with flowers."

"You little flower yerself."

140

Like that.

I was at the restaurant early and got them under the table — fast. The manageress said,

"Oh, I'll put them in water."

"No need . . . honest."

When she asked if I'd like a drink, I said,

"A beer . . . no . . . I mean . . . a Coke."

Sweat was cascading down my body.

Ann looked . . . gorgeous. There's no other word. I felt my mouth go dry, my heart pound. Stood up, said as if inspired,

"Ann."

She gave me a huge hug, then stood back to study, said,

"The beard is lovely."

"Thanks."

"You look completely different, it's not just the beard."

Not knowing what else to do, I reached for the flowers. Wow, were they a hit!

We sat.

She kept glancing at the flowers then at me. If I had to reach for how I felt, I'd have to admit, shy. Nearly fifty years old and feeling that. She said,

"I think I'm a bit shy."

"Me too."

"Oh are you, Jack? I'm delighted."

A waitress came and we ordered up a storm

Chow meins

Dim sum

Sweet and sour

Then the waitress asked,

"To drink?"

I got right to it, said,

"I'll have another Coke . . . Ann?"

"Oh, Coke for me too."

After she'd gone, Ann said,

"That's it, your eyes, they're white."

"White?"

"No, I mean . . . clear."

"It's OK, I know what you mean."

A silence. Then she said,

"Should I ask or . . . leave it alone?"

"I'm new to this myself, but sure, ask away."

"Is it difficult?"

"A bit."

Then the food came and we moved on and away. I liked to watch her eat. She caught me, asked,

"What?"

"I like to watch you eat."

"That's a good thing, isn't it?"

"I'd say so."

After, we took a walk down Quay Street. She linked my arm. Among good gestures, it's right up there. At Jury's, we stopped and she said,

"I have to go to the cemetery now. I go every day, and on such a wonderful day, I'd like to share it with Sarah."

"I'll come with you."

"Would you?"

"It would be a privilege."

Caught a cab at Dominick Street, and we were no sooner settled than the driver asked,

"You heard about the scene on the square?"

Ann said,

"Oh, wasn't it awful?"

I said nothing. The driver, of course, was contrary, said,

"People are fed up with the guards and the courts. They've had enough."

Ann was having none, said,

"Oh, surely you don't condone what happened."

"Listen, ma'am, if you saw the yokes that get in here at night and the carry on of them."

"But to set fire to a person."

"Weren't they the same pups doing that to winos? Even the guards know that."

"All the same."

"Now, ma'am, with all due respect, if something happened to *your* child."

RECIPE FOR THE UPBRINGING OF A POET:
"As much neurosis as the child can bear."

W. H. Auden

We walked to Sarah's grave in silence. She was no longer linking me.

More's the Irish pity. I could have done with it most then.

The grave was incredibly well kept. A simple wooden marker with her name. All round were

> Bears
> Snoopy
> Sweets
> Bracelets

And arranged in formation.

Said Ann,

"Her friends. They're always bringing her things."

I think that was the heartbreaker of all. I said,

"Ann, let her have the roses."

She lit up.

"Really, Jack, you don't mind? She loves roses . . . or loved. I can't get the tense right. How can I consign her to that awful one, the past?"

She laid the roses gently down and then sat near the cross. She said,

"I'm going to have *POET* put on the stone. Just that. She wanted to be one so badly."

I wasn't sure of the etiquette of the dead. Did I kneel or sit? Then, I realised Ann was talking to her child. Soft, easy sounds that reverberated against my soul.

I backed away. Started to walk and nearly collided with an elderly couple who said,

"Grand day, isn't it?"

Jesus. I kept going and arrived at my father's grave. I said,

"Dad, I'm here by default, but then . . . aren't we all?"

No doubt, I was raving. If Sutton saw me, he'd have force-fed me drink. The headstone was up and that's the worst. It's so final, no more appeals. Least while it's only the plain cross, it stays temporary.

Ann arrived behind me, asked,

"Your dad?"

I nodded.

"Did you like him?"

"Oh God, I did."

"What was he like?"

"Well, I don't think I ever wanted to be him, but I did want to be liked the way people liked him."

"What did he work at?"

"On the railways. Those days, it wasn't a bad job. Every evening round nine, he'd get his cap and go for a few pints. Two pints. Some nights he wouldn't bother. The test of an alcoholic is, if you take two daily and leave it at that. Me, I'd wait the week and have fourteen on Friday."

She gave an uncertain smile.

The talk was on me now. Rabid.

"When I joined the guards, he didn't comment except, 'Mind it doesn't lead you to drink.' Then when I got bumped, he said, 'The manner of your departure befits you better than past glories.' Early on, in Templemore, an instructor said, 'We can safely assume Taylor has a bright future behind him.' What you'd call a 'gas man'. He's a minder for the taoiseach now, so he got his just deserts. My father loved to read, was always on about the power of print. After he died, a fella stopped me in the street, said, 'Your father was a hoor for books.'

I should have put it on his stone. He'd have been happy with that."

Then I was near spent. But a thought or two to stagger home. I said,

"I have a friend, Sutton. He used to wear a t-shirt that read:

IF ARROGANCE IS A BLESSING
BEHOLD THE HOLY CITY."

Ann didn't get it, said,

"I don't understand it."

"Nor would you understand him. I don't think I do either."

Ann asked if I'd like to come visit her house. I said, sure.

She lived in Newcastle Park. Right by the hospital. A road comes out from the mortuary and it's named the Mass Path. I don't know could I walk that too often.

The house was modern, bright, clean and comfortable. It had the lived-in look. She said,

"I'll make some tea."

Which she did, emerging with a tray piled high with sandwiches. Good old-fashioned type with thick crusty bread, lashings of ham, tomato, butter. I said,

"God, those look good."

"I get the bread in Griffin's. It's always packed."

After a second cup of tea, I said,

"Ann, I have to talk to you."

"Oh, it sounds ominous."

"It's about the investigation."

"You'll need money. I have more."

"Sit down. I don't need money. I had a . . . pharmaceutical windfall, so don't worry. Look, if I told you the man responsible for Sarah's death was dead, could you be satisfied with that?"

"How do you mean. Is he?"

"Yes."

She stood up, said,

"But nobody knows. I mean, she's still classed a suicide. I can't leave her friends, her school, believing she did that."

"OK."

"OK? What does that mean, Jack? Can you prove the truth."

"I don't know."

It meant I'd have to go after Planter. If she had agreed with what I proposed, I'd have left it alone.

I think.

But Sutton certainly wasn't going to let him off, so I don't think I had any choice.

"I haven't any morals to preach.
I just work as closely to my nerves
as I can."

Francis Bacon

Later in the evening, we'd gone to bed. I was as nervous as a cat. Told her, said,

"I don't think I've ever made love sober."

"It will be better, you'll see."

It was.

Round midnight, I got dressed and Ann asked,

"Why don't you stay?"

"Not yet."

"OK."

Then she was out of bed and gone. Back a few minutes later, carrying something. She said,

"I want you to look at something."

"Sure."

"It's Sarah's diary."

And offered a pink, leather-bound book. I physically recoiled, said,

"Jesus, Ann, I can't."

"Why not?"

"I can't go through a teenage girl's diary. It's wrong."

"But why? It will give you an idea of who she is . . . who she was. Please."

"Oh God, I really don't want to do this."

I couldn't tell her that nothing would have me reaching for a bottle quicker than that. A glimpse into the mind of a young dead girl.

Ann still held it out. I said,

150

"I'll try. I can't promise I'll be able to but I'll give it a shot."

She put her arm round me, kissed my neck, said, "Thanks, Jack."

Walking home, I felt its weight like a bomb in my pocket. I thought of calling Cathy B. Asking her to read it. But I couldn't just hand it over. Ann would never go for that. Cursing like a trooper, I was home in under ten minutes. I put it under my bed so I wouldn't see it at first light. No way was I opening those pages at night.

Next morning, I showered, coffee'd, paced, then decided to face it.

The cover was well worn, the pink leather frayed from use.

Inside was:

This diary is the property of
Sarah Henderson,
Poet,
Ireland
And is PRIVATE
So no peeking, Mom!

Christ! It was worse than I thought.

Blanked my mind and tried again. A lot of the entries were predictable. School, friends, music, clothes, diets, crushes.

Was able to get through this but every so often.

Mom says I can have a mobile
phone at Christmas.
She's like the BESTEST.

And I'd want to scream.

Got to where she began work part-time at Planter's.

Mr Ford is like so un-cool.
All the girls tease him behind
his back. He is so weird city.

Then the tone changed. Now she was excited, flushed, enraptured.

152

Bart asked if I'd like a lift home.
His car is mega. I have like the
biggest crush.

Then Bart . . . just the name . . . or a heart with Bart
and Sarah . . . for pages.

The final entry:

I can't keep this diary any more.
Bart says it's for children. He's
promised me a gold bracelet if I
go to the party on Friday.

I got on the phone, called Cathy. She said,

"Where the hell have you been?"

"Undercover."

"Under the bleeding weather."

"That, too."

"You'll be wanting some-fink?"

"Pretty simple thing."

"Yeah."

"When you did research on Planter, did you keep notes?"

"Course."

"Good girl. What's his first name?"

"Lemme check."

Then,

"Got them, let's see . . . oh yeah, here it is . . . Bart
. . . holomew."

"Great!"

"Don't go yet. Listen, I've got a gig."

"Terrific, when?"

"This Saturday, at The Roisín; will you come?"

"Definitely. Can I bring somebody?"

"Bring hundreds."

A GALWAY LAMENT

You watched — through
April
from
a place of
forbearance
    . . . called fortitude.

The Roisín Dubh has showcased most of the major music acts. It still retains the atmosphere of intimacy. Read crowded. Ann was wearing a short leather jacket, faded 501's, her hair tied back. I said,

"Now, that's gig gear."

"Is it OK?"

"Dynamite."

I'd faded to black. Sweatshirt and cords in that colour. Ann said,

"You look like a spoilt priest."

"Petulant?"

"No, spoilt as in . . . ruined."

"Mm . . . we could work on that."

We squeezed through the crowd, got near the stage. I said,

"Listen, I'm just going to see how Cathy's doing."

"Will she be nervous?"

"I am."

Cathy was in a tiny dressing room, said,

"I knew you'd come."

"Yeah?"

"Sure, you still have some moves, even for an old guy. Here . . ."

She pushed a glass at me, it was a double, no a treble something. I asked,

"What's that?"

"Jack . . . as in Daniels. Get you kick-started."

"No, thanks."

"What!"

"I'm not drinking."

She turned round, said,

"You what?"

"Been a few days. I'm working at it."

"Wow!"

I'd have given my back teeth for it. The light seemed to catch the glass, made the liquid sparkle. I looked away. Cathy asked,

"And the beard? What's with that?"

"Notions."

"That's an Irish answer. Tells me absolutely zero. Go . . . I need to focus."

I bent down, kissed the top of her head, said,

"Star trouper."

Ann was holding drinks, said,

"Cokes . . . I didn't mean to presume."

"Coke is great."

Various people shouted hello, commented on the beard, scrutinised Ann.

Lights went down and I thought I spotted Sutton near the bar.

Then Cathy was up. The crowd went quiet. She said,

"Hello."

"Hello yourself."

Straight into a punk version of "Galway Bay". Like when Sid Vicious did "My Way". Difference being that Cathy could sing. Gave the song a poignancy I'd lost over too many hearings. Next came Neil Young's "Powderfinger".

156

She covered a huge range, from Chrissie Hynde through Alison Moyet, to conclude with Margo Timmins' "Misguided Angel". Stormed through that. Then she was gone. Huge applause, whistles, calls for more. I said to Ann,

"She won't do an encore."

"Why."

"Never keeps a reserve — she's done."

She was.

The lights came up. A wave of camaraderie, good will pervaded the place. Ann said,

"She's brilliant. What a voice."

"Drink? Have a real one, I'm OK truly."

"White wine."

"Sure."

When I got it, I turned to find Sutton blocking my path. He looked at the glass, said,

"Wine? It's a start."

"Not for me."

"Whatever. That English chick can sure belt it out. I'd say she'd murder you in bed."

"Not your type."

"They're all my type. You'll remember our Mr Planter?"

"Sure."

"He does admire painters. Fancies himself a collector."

"You spoke to him."

"Lovely man. I'm due at his place at noon tomorrow. You can come as my assistant."

"What are you planning?"

"To frame the fuck. I'm a painter, Jack. Remember? I'll pick you up at 11.30."

I gave Ann her drink, said,

"I'll just say goodbye to Cathy."

"Tell her she was mighty."

A true Galway description, the highest accolade. Cathy's dressing room was jammed with admirers, her face was flushed, her eyes alight. I said,

"You were sensational."

"Thanks, Jack."

"Listen, you're busy, I just wanted to let you know."

"Keep the beard."

"You think?"

"Makes you look like you've got character."

A snake had bitten so many people that few ventured out.

The Master was credited with taming the snake. As a result, the people took to throwing stones and dragging it by its tail.

The snake complained to the Master, who said, "You've stopped frightening people, that's bad."

A very pissed-off snake replied,

"You told me to practise non-violence."

"No, I told you to stop hurting — not to stop hissing."

Next morning, I actually made breakfast. Not being sick, hung over, was extraordinary. My face was healing and the beard hid the rest. Fixed a mess of eggs and cut a wedge of thick bread. I'd been to Griffin's.

Full mug of tea and I was set. My door went and I said,

"Shit."

It was Sutton. I said,

"Jeez, how early is this?"

"Man, I haven't been to bed."

"Come in, have some breakfast."

He followed me in and I went to grab another plate. He said,

"I'll drink mine, thanks."

"All I've got is some cheap Scotch."

"I'm a cheap guy. Gimme a coffee to colour it."

My eggs had gone cold. After I got him the coffee and Scotch bottle, he indicated my plate, said,

"Tell me you're not going to eat that."

"Now I'm not. I've got this fetish, I like to eat my grub with some semblance of heat."

"Whoo . . . testy."

He looked round the flat, said,

"I could be happy here."

"What?"

"I was round the other day, but you were off gallivanting. I got to chatting to your neighbour, Laura."

160

"Linda."

"Whatever. A thick country wan with all that low cunning. I, of course, charmed the pants off her. Not literally, of course. Once she knew I was an artist, she offered me your flat."

"She offered what?"

"Is there an echo here? Yeah, said you were moving and she was looking for a suitable tenant."

"The bad bitch."

"The attraction of art, eh?"

"Are you serious, you're going to move in?"

He stood up, slurped off the coffee, gave me a wide-eyed look, said,

"Hey big buddy. Would I shaft you? You're my main man. We better go, art beckons."

A beat up VW Golf was parked outside. A bright yellow colour. I said,

"Say it isn't so."

"Oh yeah. The Volvo is shagged. I had to borrow this."

"They'll literally see us coming."

"Course they will."

Planter lived in Oughterard. His house on the approach into the village. House is too tame a term. Obviously, he'd seen Dallas too often and decided to have an Irish Southfork. I said,

"Jeez."

"But are we impressed?"

A lengthy tree-lined drive, then the main house. More garish close up. Sutton said,

"I'll do the talking."

"That should be a novelty."

He rang the bell, and I noticed security cameras above the portals. The door opened, a young woman in a maid's uniform asked,

"Que?"

Sutton gave his best smile, all demonic dazzle, said,

"*Buenas dias, señorita*, I am *Señor* Sutton, *el artist*."

She gave a nervous giggle, waved us in. I looked at Sutton, asked,

"You speak Spanish?"

"I do spick."

She led us into a lavish study, said,

"*Momento, por favor*."

Paintings lined every wall. Sutton gave them a close inspection, said,

"Some good stuff here."

A voice said,

"Glad you approve."

We turned.

Planter was standing at the door. I'm not sure what I expected, but with the house, the business, the reputation, I'd imagined a big man. He wasn't. Came in at 5'5" or so, almost bald with a heavily lined face. His eyes were dark, revealing little. Dressed in a sweater with a polo logo and very shabby cords. You knew he'd have a worn-to-shit Barbour jacket for outdoors. Nobody offered handshakes. The atmosphere couldn't hold it. Sutton said,

"I'm Sutton and Jack here is my assistant."

Planter nodded, asked,

"Some refreshment?"

162

Then he clapped his hands and the maid returned. Sutton said,

"*Dos cervezas.*"

We stood in silence till she returned with the two beers on a tray. Sutton took both, said,

"Jack won't be partaking. I don't pay the help to drink."

Planter gave a brief smile, said,

"Please be seated."

He marched over to a leather armchair. I checked to see if his feet reached the floor. Sutton sat opposite and I remained standing. Planter said,

"I have been an admirer of your work for some time. The idea of a commission attracts me."

Sutton had finished one beer, belched, said,

"How about a portrait?"

"You do portraits?"

"Not yet but a few more beers, I'd paint Timbuktu."

Planter wasn't bothered by Sutton's manner. On the contrary, he seemed to find it amusing, said,

"No doubt. I think perhaps a landscape."

I said,

"What about water?"

He was taken aback, had to turn to face me, asked,

"I beg your pardon?"

"Water, Bartholomew; you don't mind if I call you that? How about Nimmo's Pier, serve to jog your memory?"

He was up, said,

"I'd like you to leave now."

Sutton said,

163

"I could go another beer."

"Shall I call help?"

I said,

"No, we'll see ourselves out. But we'll be in touch, about Nimmo's."

I miss a lot of things
but most of all
I miss myself.

Outside Planter's house, I said to Sutton,

"Gimme the car keys."

"I can drive."

"What if that prick calls the guards?"

I was never a great driver. With my left hand bandaged, I was close to dangerous. Still, a better option than the sodden Sutton. I ground the gears a few times and Sutton roared,

"You'll burn out the clutch."

"You said the car was borrowed."

"Borrowed, not disposable."

I took it slow, tried to ignore the impatience of other drivers. Sutton said,

"You fucked that good."

"Come again?"

"Planter! I thought we agreed you'd keep your mouth shut."

"I don't do hired help good."

"I wanted to play, fuck with his head more."

"We fucked his head all right. Just a bit sooner is all."

"What's the plan now?"

"Let's wait and see."

"That's the plan?"

"I didn't say it was a good plan, just the only one."

Back in Galway, eventually. Sutton had nodded off. I stirred him and he came to with a jump, saying,

"What the fuck!"

"Take it away, we're in town."

"Man, I'd a rough dream. Tobe Hopper would be proud of it. My mouth feels like a canary shit in it."

"Do you want to come in, grab a shower?"

"Naw, I'm for the *leaba*."

I got out and waited. Sutton shook himself, said,

"Jack, you wouldn't ever think of selling me out?"

"What?"

"'Cause I wouldn't like that. You 'n' me, we're tied together."

"Who'd I sell you out to?"

"The guards. You know the old saying . . . once a garda! You might want to score some points with your old mates."

"That's mad talk."

He gave a long look, then,

"You're shaping up to be a citizen, you know that. God knows, you were some fuck-up drinking, but at least you were predictable."

"Get some sleep."

"And you, Jack, get some focus."

He put the car in gear, screeched into traffic. I went into the flat, tried to rustle up some breakfast again. But my heart wasn't in it. Settled for coffee and sank into a chair. I considered what he'd said and wondered if there was any truth in his accusations. One drink and that would burn any righteous notions. Burn everything else, too.

I thought about Planter and couldn't see how I was going to prove he was responsible for Sarah's death.

Time was running out, too, on my accommodation. If I was going to be homeless, at least I had the beard for it.

The next few days, I heard nothing from Sutton. Checked at the Skeff but no sign. Went into Grogan's and Sean provided the real coffee. I asked,

"What? No biscuit?"

"You don't need back-up no more."

"Sean."

"What?"

"You've known me . . . how long?"

"Donkeys."

"Right. You've seen me in all kinds of states."

"That I have."

"So, all told, you know me better than anyone."

"Too true."

"Would you say I'd be capable of selling out a friend?"

If he was surprised by the question, he didn't show it. Seemed to give it serious thought. I'd been expecting an immediate "course not". Finally he looked me right in the eye, said,

"Well, you used to be a guard."

And I have held your hand
for reasons
not at all.

In reality, time doesn't pass. We pass. I have no idea why, but I think that's one of the saddest things I ever learnt. God knows, anything I have learnt has been the hard way.

An alcoholic's greatest defect is a complete unwillingness to learn from the past.

What I knew from mine was if I drank, chaos reigned. I was no longer under any illusion. Yet I'd have given anything to crack the seal on a bottle of Scotch and fly. Or even, a feast of pints. Close my eyes and there was a table. Wooden, of course. Dozens of creamy Guinness lined in greeting. The head . . . ahhh, just perfect.

Stood up and physically shook myself. This was eating me alive. Galway's a great walking town. Walking the prom is the favoured route. Used to be only Galwegians followed a particular ritual. You started at Grattan Road, then up past Seapoint. Stop a moment there and hear the ghost of all the showbands past:

> The Royal
> Dixies
> Howdowners
> The Miami

I can't say if it was a simple age. But it was a whole lot less complicated. In the middle of a jive, no mobile phone blew away the magic. Then on past Claude Toft's, along the beach till you reached Blackrock.

170

Here's where the ritual kicked in. At the wall, you touched it with your shoe.

Word is out though. Even the Japanese aim a semi-karate shot to the stone.

I don't begrudge them the act, but somehow it's been diluted.

Go figure.

I walked into town and decided to get a blast of caffeine for the trip.

As long as I remember, there's been sentries. Two men who perch on stools at any given hour. Always the same duo. They wear cloth caps, donkey jackets and terylene pants. Never together. They sit at opposite ends of the bar. I wouldn't swear they even knew each other.

Now here's the thing.

No matter how you sneak up on these guys or what way you approach them, it never changes. Two pint glasses of Guinness, half full. It's synchronicity gone ape. You couldn't plan it. Some day, to walk in and see either full glasses or even empty, then I'll know change is here to stay.

As I headed for my usual seat, I glanced to check. Yup, the two in place, halves at the ready.

Sean was as contrary as a bag of cats. Plonked coffee down in front of me, saying nothing. I said,

"And a good morning to you, too."

"Don't get lippy with me."

Suitably chastised, I sipped the coffee. Not so hot, but I felt it wasn't the morning to mention it. I glanced at the paper. Read how the gardaí wouldn't be part of a

171

new EU force as they weren't armed. A fellow I vaguely knew approached, asked,

"Might I have a word, Jack?"

"Sure, sit down."

"I dunno do you remember me. I'm Phil Joyce."

"Course I do."

I didn't.

He sat and produced tobacco and papers, asked,

"Hope you don't mind."

"Fire away."

He did.

He was one of those skull smokers. Sucked the nicotine in so hard it made his cheekbones bulge. He blew out the smoke with a deep sigh. Whether contentment or agony, it was a close call. He said,

"I knew you better when you were doing your line."

God be with the days. Doing a line was all but redundant. Then, you met a girl, went to the pictures, for walks and, if you were lucky, held her hand for reasons not at all. Now, it was "a relationship" and you were ambushed at every stage by

> issues
> empowerment
> and
> the inner child

The only lines now were of cocaine.

You didn't bring flowers any more, you brought a therapist. He said,

"I heard you were off the gargle."

"A bit."

"Good man. Will you give me a reference?"

"For what?"

"The Post Office."

"Sure, but I'm not sure I'm the best choice."

"Oh, that doesn't matter, I don't want the job."

"Excuse me?"

"Keep the Social Welfare off me back. Look like I'm trying."

"Um . . . OK."

"Right, thanks a lot."

Then he was gone. I stood up and made to leave money on the table. Sean was over, asked,

"What's that?"

"The price of the coffee."

"Oh . . . and since when did you start paying?"

I'd had it, barked,

"What sort of bug is up your arse?"

"Watch your language, young Taylor."

I brushed past him, said,

"You're a cranky oul bastard."

At a recent mass in Galway Cathedral, a young New Age traveller horrified the congregation by walking up the aisle waving a replica gun.

He was charged but released on bail of 6p, because he was broke.

His New Age friends, locals later discovered, had tamed eleven rats that they christened and cared for in their tents.

Like the guy in the Carlsberg commercial, one can only ask, "Why?"

I was heading down Quay Street. Hardened locals pronounce it "Kay" and it's "Key" to the rest. A rib must have been broken in the devil as a shard of sun hit the buildings.

A shadow fell. The head wino. I knew him as Padraig. The usual rumours beset him. Supposedly from a good family, he had been

A teacher

A lawyer

A brain surgeon

As long as I'd known him, he was in bits and fond of the literary allusion. Today, he was semi-pissed, said,

"And greetings to you, my bearded friend. Are we perchance partaking of the late winter solstice?"

I smiled and gave him a few quid. The tremoring of his hand we both ignored. He was about 5′5″ in height, emaciated, with a mop of dirty white hair. The face was a riot of broken blood vessels, swollen now. The nose was broken and I could sure empathise.

Blue, the bluest eyes you'd ever get . . . underlined in red, of course. Ordnance surveyed. He said,

"Did I know your father?"

"Paddy . . . Paddy Taylor."

"A man of subtlety and taste. Was he not?"

"He had his moments."

"One deduces from the use of the past tense that he's no longer with us — or worse — in England."

175

"Dead, he's dead."

At the top of his lungs. Padraig began to sing. It put the heart crossways in me. He sang or roared,

Blindly, blindly
at last
do we pass away.

He stooped to snatch a fag end, lit it from a battered box of kitchen matches. I looked furtively round, hoping the song was through. He ate deep from the cigarette and in a cloud of nicotine bellowed,

But man may not linger
for nowhere
finds he repose.

He paused and I jumped in.

"Will you stop if I give you more money?"

He laughed, showing two yellowed teeth; the rest, obviously, were casualties of combat.

"Indeed I will."

I gave him another pound. He examined it, said,

"I take Euros, too."

I was crossing into Claddagh with the Spanish Arch to my left. Padraig continued to match stride, said,

"You are not a man who gives away a lot . . . a lot, that is, in the information department. What you do say has the qualities of brevity and clarity."

Before I could reply to this, briefly or clearly, he was assailed with a series of gut wrenching coughs. Up

176

came phlegm and various unidentifiable substances. I gave him a handkerchief. He used it to dry his streaming eyes.

"I am indebted to you, young Taylor. It has been many the mile since I was offered a fellow pilgrim's hanky."

I said,

"Your accent is hard to pin down."

"Like a steady income, it has an elusive quality . . . not to mention effusive."

There was no reply to this, I didn't even try. He said,

"At one dark era of my existence I was, I believe, from the countryside of Louth. Are you at all familiar with that barren territory?"

"No."

My concentration was focused on not talking like him. It was highly contagious. He rooted deep in his coat, a heavy tweed number. Out came a brown bottle.

"A touch of biddy perhaps?"

He wiped the neck with the clean end of my hanky. I shook my head. He wasn't the least offended, said,

"The only advice I remember is it's better to be lucky than good."

"And are you?"

"What?"

"Lucky?"

He laughed deep.

"It has been a long time, anyway, since I was any good. Whatever that means."

A bunch of winos emerged from the football wall. Padraig shook himself in artificial energy, said,

"My people await me. Perchance we'll talk again."

"I'd like that."

Not wild enthusiasm but a certain tone of approval.

Finally, I made Salthill and hit out along the prom. I thought again about the sentries in Grogan's. Any given day, come noon, they took off their caps, blessed themselves for the angelus. Even bowed their heads as they quietly whispered the prayer.

Save for those odd pockets of remembrance, the angelus, like the tenements and pawn shop of Quay Street, had been blown away by the new prosperity. Who's to measure the loss? I couldn't even recall the prayer.

When you come off the booze, you acquire a racing mind. A hundred thoughts assail you at once.

Three lads in their barely twenties passed me. They were holding cans of Tenants Super. I could have mugged them. The smell of the lager called loud.

I'd come across some books by Keith Ablow. A practising psychiatrist with a specialty in forensics, he wrote,

You need a drink. That's how it starts. You need. And the need was real, always is. Because I did need something. I needed the courage to face what I had to do next. And I didn't have it. The booze makes you forget that you're a coward, for a while. Until a while runs out. Whatever you needed to face has grown claws and become a monster you don't ever want to meet. Then the monster starts pissing out booze faster than you can pour it in.

Walk that.

Remember the primary laws of physics: every force begets an equal and opposite force. If you perform an act of grace, you buck the system. It's like throwing down the gauntlet to Satan. All kinds of hell can come looking for you.

Next day, invigorated from my walk, I decided to get my hand checked.

I had a doctor, but over the years of drink, I'd lost contact. Once, I'd gone to score some heavy duty tranquillisers and he ran me.

I didn't even know if he was still alive. Took the chance and went to the Crescent.

A pit stop connecting the seaside and the city. It's the Harley Street of the town. His nameplate was still there. Went in and a young receptionist asked,

"Can I help you?"

"I used to be a patient, but I dunno if I'm still on the books."

"Let's see, shall we."

I was.

She glanced through the file, said,

"Ah, you're with the gardaí."

Jeez, how long since I'd been? She looked at my beard and I said,

"Undercover."

She didn't believe that for a second, said,

"I'll check if the doctor's free."

He was.

He'd gotten old, but then, who hadn't? He said,

"My word, you've been in the wars."

"I have."

Gave me a full examination, said,

"Fingers can come out of plaster in a few weeks. The nose you're stuck with. What about the alcohol?"

"I'm off it."

"Time for you. They measure alcohol in units now. How many per day? I'm old school, I suppose; I measure how many people it puts in units."

I didn't know if this was humour so let it slide. Dismissing me, he said,

"God bless."

I didn't go to Grogan's, thought,

"Today I can live without Sean's tongue."

Met Linda outside my flat and she reminded me.

"You have two weeks to find a new place."

I thought of a range of answers but decided on confusion, said,

"God bless."

I was watching Sky Sports that evening when the phone rang. It was Ann. I breezed,

"Hi, honey."

"Jack, there's been an accident, a bad one."

"What? Who?"

"It's Sean . . . he's dead."

"Oh God!"

"Jack . . . Jack, I'm at the hospital. They have Sean here."

"Wait there, I'll come."

I put the phone down. Then drew back my left hand, punched the wall. The force against my mending fingers made me scream. Four, five times, I systematically pounded the wall then slumped from the pain. A howl of anguish terrified me till I realised I was making the sound.

Ann was waiting at the hospital entrance. She made to hug me but I waved her away. She saw my hand, asked,

"What happened?"

"I fell and no, I wasn't drinking."

"I didn't mean . . ."

I took her hand in my right one, said,

"I know you didn't. Where is he? What happened?"

"It was a hit and run. They say he died instantaneously."

"How do they know?"

On the third floor a doctor and two gardaí. The doctor asked,

"Are you family?"

"I dunno."

The gardaí exchanged a look. I asked,

"Can I see him?"

The doctor looked at Ann, said,

"I don't think that's a good idea."

"Do I know you?"

He shook his head and I continued,

"That's what I thought, so how the hell would you know?"

One of the gardaí said,

"Hey."

The doctor said,

"Come with me."

He led me down the corridor, stopped in a doorway, said,

"Prepare yourself. We haven't had a chance to really clean him up."

I didn't answer.

Curtains had been pulled round a bed. The doctor gave me one final glance then pulled the curtain, said,

"I'll leave you alone."

Sean was lying on his back, heavy bruising covered his forehead. Gashes ran along his face. His trousers were torn and a bony knee protruded. He was wearing a navy sweater I'd given him for Christmas. It was soiled.

I leant over him and to my horror, my tears fell on his forehead. I tried to brush them off. Then I kissed his brow and said,

"I'm not drinking, isn't that great?"

You live your life
of cold hellos
and I
being poorer
live for nothing, nothing at all.

Ann persuaded me to have my hand seen to. I got a fresh plaster and a bollocking. The nurse snapped,

"Stop breaking those fingers."

Which was definitely cutting to the chase. Ann wanted to come home with me, but I persuaded her I needed some time alone. I said,

"I'm not going to drink."

"Oh, Jack."

"I owe it to Sean."

"You owe it to yourself."

Argue that. I didn't.

I'd wrangled some painkillers. Strict instructions to only take two daily. When I got home, I popped three. In jig time I was floating. A feeling of mellow detachment. I got into bed with a working smile. Whatever I was dreaming, I was liking it.

A tugging at my shoulder dragged me reluctantly awake. Sutton stood over the bed, saying,

"Man, you were gone."

"Sutton, what the . . . how the hell did you get in?"

Even in the darkness, I could decipher the smile. He said,

"You know me, Jack, I can get in anywhere. Here, I made us some coffee."

I sat up and he pushed a mug at me. Raised it to lips and smelt the brandy. I shouted,

"What the hell is this? You've spiked it."

186

"Just to help the shock. I am so sorry about Sean."

I pushed the coffee away, got out of bed and pulled jeans on. Sutton said,

"I'll wait in the other room."

In the bathroom, I checked the mirror. My pupils were pin points. Shuddered as I thought, "What if I'd lashed brandy down on that?"

Put my head under the cold tap and let the water gush. It helped, the grogginess eased. Went out to Sutton, asked,

"When did you hear?"

"Only a little while ago. I found a place to live and was preoccupied with moving in. Sorry, Jack, I'd have been here sooner."

"Where's your place?"

"You know the hills above the Sky Road?"

"Vaguely."

"An American had a huge warehouse of a thing there. But the weather got to him. I took a year's lease. You want to come share?"

"What? No . . . I mean . . . no, thanks . . . I'm a city boy."

I noticed a stone bottle on my press, asked,

"What's that?"

"Oh, that's mine. It's Genever, Dutch gin. I'll bring it with me when I go. I just wanted to check you were OK. I know what Sean meant to you."

"Means!"

"Whatever."

We talked for a while about Sean. Sutton said,

"You really loved . . . love that old codger."

Then he stood up, said,

"I better head. If there's anything I can do, you got it
. . . understand? I'm here for you, buddy."

I nodded.

A few minutes later, I could hear him pull away. I
stayed sitting for the next half hour. My head down, my
mind near blank. Slowly, I turned round and focused
on the stone bottle. I could swear it moved. Moved
towards me. I said aloud,

"Thank Christ, I don't need that."

Began to wonder what it smelled like. Went over
and picked up the bottle. Heavy. Unscrewed the
top and took a whiff. Wow, like grain alcohol. Put
the bottle back down, without the cap, said,

"Let it breathe . . . or is that wine?'

Went into the kitchen, figured a tea with tons of
sugar would be good. A voice in the back of my mind
tried to say,

"You're in the zone."

I shut it down. Opened the cupboard and there was
the Roches glass. I said,

"No way, José," and let it crash into the sink. Didn't
break, and I said, "You stubborn bastard."

Got a hammer and pounded it to smithereens. A
piece of flying glass cut my left eyebrow. I threw the
hammer in the sink and went back to the other room.
Walked over, took the gin and drank from the neck.

"TOP
    OF
        THE
            WORLD,
                MA!"

James Cagney, *White Heat*

To keep the account balanced, I should mention my mother. Ann had said,

"You talk about your father a lot. I know you think about him all the time, but you never say anything about your mother."

"Let's keep it that way."

Terse.

My father highly rated Henry James. It was an unlikely choice. A man, working on the railway in the West of Ireland reading an American from a totally different world. He said,

"James seems so polished and stylish, but beneath there lurks . . ."

He didn't finish. That "lurks" was enticement enough to a child of darkness.

In *What Maisie Knew*, the nine-year-old child says,

"I don't think my mother cares much for me."

I *knew* my mother didn't have a lot of *grá* . . . for anyone. Least of all me. She is the very worst of things, a snob, and she's from Leitrim! Nothing and nobody ever measured up. Probably not even herself. Deep down, I might understand she's a desperately unhappy person, but I could care less.

A mouth on her.

Not a nag, a demolition expert.

Chip
Chip
Chip

away at you. Slowly eroding confidence and esteem. Her rant to me,

"You'll come to nothing like your father."

"How the mighty have fallen."

This! From Leitrim.

No wonder I drank.

"Your father's a small man, in a small uniform, with a small job."

As a child, I was afraid of her. Later, I hated her. In my twenties I despised her and now, I ignore her.

Over the past five years, I'd seen her maybe twice. Both disasters.

At some stage, she fell over Valium, and for a time she simply fell over. Took the edge offa that mouth. After that, it was a tonic wine. Mugs of the stuff. So, she'd always a buzz going.

She loved priests.

I'm going to put it on her headstone. Tells all you'd need to know. Nuns, of course, also like priests but it's mandatory. Built into their contract.

My mother always had a tame cleric in tow. Word was, the most current was Fr Malachy. He, of the Major cigarettes. She was, too, a regular churchgoer, sodality supporter, novena groupie. Times I'd seen her wear a brown scapular *outside* a blouse. A heavy hitter.

Odd moments, I have sought for her redeeming features.

There are none.

In later life, I was exactly what she needed. A wayward son who helped her to public martyrdom. How could she lose? After I was booted from the gardaí, she leaked piety from every pore. Her theme song:

"Never darken my door again."

She carried on scandalously at my father's funeral. Collapsing at the grave, wailing in the street, huge wreath of vulgar proportions.

Like that.

Course, she leapt into widow's weeds and wore black ever since. If anything, her church attendance increased. Never a kind word during his lifetime, she belied him in his death.

He had said to me,

"Your mother means well."

She didn't.

Not then, not ever.

Her type thrive on the goodness of others. The "mean well" credo excuses every despicable act of their calculated lives. I like to see photos of dictators, tyrants, warlords. Somewhere towards the back, you'll find "Mama" with a face of stone and eyes of pure granite. They are the banality of evil that people discuss and so rarely recognise.

Sean had always spoken well of her, tried to change my attitude, had said,

"She loves you, Jack, in her own way."

She stayed in touch with him, I believe, as a means of keeping tabs on me. I said to him,

"Don't, and I mean *don't* tell her anything about me . . . ever."

"Jack, she's your mother."

"I mean it, Sean."

"Arrah, you're only saying that."

After I hit the gin, I went into free-fall. I don't remember anything else till I came to in my mother's house. No wonder they call it mother's ruin.

NO

...

TO

BENEDICTION

Opened my eyes. Expecting restraints or a prison cell or both. Felt beyond ill. I was in a bed, a fresh, clean one. Tried to sit up and my heart reeled in terror. A black figure was sitting at the end of the bed. I must have shrieked; the figure spoke.

"Relax, Jack, you're safe."

Managed to focus, asked,

"Fr Malachy?"

" 'Tis."

"What? How?"

"You're at your mother's."

"Oh, Jesus."

"Don't take the Lord's name in vain."

My head was opening but I had to know.

"Are you living here?"

"Don't be an eejit. Your mother called me."

"Shit!"

"Watch that tongue, laddie. I won't abide cursing."

"So, sue me."

I noticed I was wearing pyjamas, old comfortable ones, washed a hundred times, then said,

"Oh God, I think these are my father's."

"May he rest in peace. Though I fear he'd turn in his grave at your antics."

I managed to sit on the side of the bed, asked,

"Any chance of tea?"

He shook his head sadly. I asked,

"What? Tea's beyond your brief?"

"You were a holy show you know. Swearing at your mother. By the time I got here, you'd passed out."

I tried to assemble my shattered mind. Could dredge up that it was Friday night when I'd drunk. Took a deep breath asked,

"What day is this?"

He gave me a look of almost pity, asked,

"You really don't know?"

"Sure, I'd ask for the sheer hell of it."

"It's Wednesday."

I sank my head in my hands. I was going to need a cure and soon. Malachy said,

"Sean was buried yesterday."

"Was I there?"

"No."

I so badly needed to throw up and maintain it for a week. Malachy added,

"Sean's son, named I think William, came home from England. He'll be taking over the pub. Seems a sensible lad."

Malachy stood up, looked at his watch, said,

"I have a mass. I trust you'll do the right thing by your mother."

"You're not smoking, have you quit?"

"God hasn't seen fit to relieve me of that particular burden yet, but I wouldn't dream of smoking in your mother's house."

"Blame God, eh?"

"I didn't say that."

"Why not? I blame him all the time."

"And look at the cut of you. It's no wonder."
Then he was gone. My clothes were

> Washed
>
> Ironed
>
> Folded

at the end of the bed.

I struggled into them. Took a while as bouts of nausea engulfed me. Taking a deep breath, I headed downstairs. She was in the kitchen, doing kitchen things. I said,

"Hi."

She turned to face me. My mother has good strong features but they're arranged wrong. They add up to severity. If we get the face we deserve by the time we're forty, then she got the jackpot. Deep lines on her forehead and at the sides of her nose. Her hair was gray and pulled right back in an impossible knot. But the eyes told all, a direct unyielding dark brown. Whatever else they said, "no prisoners" was the overriding message. She said,

"So, you're up."

"Yes . . . I'm . . . sorry . . . for . . . you know, the disturbance."

She sighed. It was what she did best. She could have sighed for Ireland, said,

"Oh, I'm well used to it."

I had to sit down. She asked,

"You'll be expecting something?"

"What?"

"Breakfast."

"Oh, I'd love some tea."

197

As she filled a kettle, I glanced round. To her left, I saw a bottle of Buckfast. It would do. I said,

"The doorbell's ringing."

"What?"

"Yeah, it rang twice."

"I didn't hear it."

"You probably couldn't hear it over the kettle."

She went. I was up and over to the bottle, got a huge belt of it. Christ, it was rough, thought, "People buy this shit by choice?"

The moment of truth, would it stay down or up. Hit my stomach like battery acid. Went back to my chair and waited. Began to settle, could feel that glow in my guts. My mother was back, suspicion writ large, said,

"There wasn't anyone."

"Oh."

She looked like a warden who knows there's been an escape but who doesn't know who's gone. I stood, said,

"Think I'll skip the tea."

"But the kettle's boiled."

"I'll have to go."

"Are you still working . . . as . . ."

She couldn't bring herself to finish. I said,

"I am."

"And you're looking at some girl's suicide?"

"How do you know? . . . oh, Fr Malachy."

"Arrah, the whole town knows. Though God knows how you find the time between drinking."

I got to the door, said,

"Thanks again."

She put her hands on her hips, looked set to charge, said, "Well it would be a quare thing if you couldn't come to your own home."

"This was never home."

KARMA

Walking down College Road, I thought I probably should have said something kinder. Years ago I'd read where a man asks,

How come, no matter how long since I've seen the family or how much distance I put between us, they can always push my buttons?

The answer:

Because they installed them.

At the Fair Green, I was hit by a dizzy spasm and had to lean against a wall. Two women passing gave me a wide berth, one said,

"Elephants, and it's not eleven yet."

Sweat cascaded down my face. A hand touched my shoulder. I felt so bad I hoped I was being mugged. A voice,

"You're in some distress, my friend."

That distinctive tone. It was Padraig, the head wino. He took my arm, said,

"There's a bench here, far from the madding crowd."

Led me down. I thought, if my mother's watching, as she always was, she'd hardly be surprised. Got to the seat and Padraig said,

"Here, attempt a sip of this potion."

I looked at a brown bottle and he said,

"Can it be any worse than what you've already imbibed?"

"Good point."

I drank. If anything it was tasteless. I'd expected meths. He said,

"You expected meths."

I nodded.

"This is an emergency concoction I learned from the British army."

"You were in the army?"

"I don't know. Somedays, I would swear I still am."

Already, I was improving, said,

"It's doing the job."

"*Certainement*. The British understand the concept of relief. They don't, alas, always know where it applies."

This was way beyond me so I said nothing. He asked,

"To paraphrase our American allies, you tied one on?"

"Whoooo . . . did I ever."

"Was there an occasion?"

"My friend died."

"Ah, my condolences."

"I missed his funeral and, no doubt, pissed off what few friends I had."

A garda came, stood and barked,

"Ye'll have to move along, this is a public area."

Padraig was up before I could answer, said,

"Yes, officer, we're on our way."

202

As we moved, I said to Padraig,

"Jumped up gobshite."

Padraig gave a small smile, said,

"There's a pugnacious streak in you."

"I know those guys. I used to be one."

"A gobshite?"

I laughed despite myself.

"Well, probably. But I used to be a garda."

He was surprised, stopped, took my measure, said,

"Now that I wouldn't have surmised."

"It was a long time ago."

"One senses a certain longing though. Perhaps you might reapply."

"I don't think so. These days, they like candidates to have a degree."

"But a degree of what."

We'd reached the top of the square. A drinking school near the toilets called to Padraig. I said,

"Before you go, can I ask you something?"

"Verily. I cannot promise an answer of truth, but I'll try for conviction."

"Do you believe in karma?"

He put a finger to his lips, didn't answer for ages, then,

"For every action there is an equal and opposite reaction . . . yes, I believe."

"Then I'm fucked."

"The challenge to each human is creation. Will you create with reverence, or with neglect?"

Gary Zukav, *The Seat of the Soul*

I'd gotten home with only a six pack. At the off-licence, I'd wanted to lash in the Scotch but if I had any chance, that wasn't it. Padraig's potion had held and I got to bed without further damage.

Slept till dawn. Coming to, I wasn't in the first circle of hell. Was able to forgo the cure and get some coffee down. Sure, I was shaky as bejaysus but nothing new in that. Put the sixer in the fridge and hoped I could ration down. Showered till my skin stung and even trimmed the full arrived beard. Checked the mirror and went,

"Phew"

The reflection showed a tattered face.

Phoned Ann. Answered on first ring.

"Yes."

"Ann, it's Jack."

"Yes?"

Ice.

"Ann, I don't know where to begin."

"Don't bother."

"What?"

"I'm not able for this any more. I'll send you a cheque for your services, I won't be requiring them further."

"Ann . . . please."

"Your friend is in Rahoon Cemetery. Not far from Sarah. If you're ever sober enough to get there. Personally, I doubt even that."

"Could I just . . ."

"I don't want to hear it. Please don't call me again."

The phone went down. I struggled into my suit and headed out. At the cathedral, I heard my name being called. A man came running over, said,

"I got it."

"What?"

"The Post Office. I gave you as a reference."

"I thought you didn't want the job."

"I don't, but it's nice to be wanted."

"Well, I'm glad. When do you start?"

"Start what?"

"The job."

He looked at me as if I was nuts, said,

"I'm not going to take it."

"Oh."

"Anyway, I have a horse for you."

By this stage, I half expected he'd trot a stallion out from the church. He said,

"The 3.30 at Ayr. Rocket Man. Take a price and go heavy."

"How heavy?"

"Feckin' medieval."

"OK . . . thanks."

"Thank you. I always wanted to be a postman."

Stopped in Javas for a coffee. The waitress had no English but a dazzling smile. That's a fair trade. I said,

"Double espresso."

Pointed it out on the menu.

Moment of financial truth. Took out my wallet and gave the first sigh of relief. It wasn't weightless. Had a peek. Notes . . . notes were visible. Slow to slower count, one in fact to count cadence. Two hundred. Before I could rejoice, a shadow fell across me.

A large man, familiar if not instantly recognisable. He asked,

"Might I have a word?"

I put my left hand on the table, said,

"Come to break them again."

It was the guy from the security firm, the guard who'd given me my original beating. He pulled out a chair, said,

"I want to explain."

The waitress brought the coffee, looked at him, but he waved her away. I said,

"This I've got to hear."

He began.

"You know I'm a guard. The security is a good nixer, lots of the lads do it. When Mr Ford told me you were causing trouble, I helped out. I didn't realise what he was. He's dead, did you know?"

"I heard."

"Yeah, well, turns out he was a pervert. Hand on my heart, I'd never stomach that. After . . . after we'd done you . . . I found out you used to be on the force. If I'd known . . . I swear, I'd never have done it."

"What is it you want, forgiveness?"

He lowered his head.

"I've been reborn in the Spirit."

"How nice."

"No, it's true. I've resigned from the force and the security. I'm going to do God's work now."

I sipped the espresso. Bitter as unheard prayer. He said,

"I hear you're still on that case, the young girl's suicide."

"Yeah."

"I want to help. To make amends."

He produced a piece of paper, said,

"This is my phone number. I still have contacts, and if you need anything . . ."

"I'll have God on my side, is that it?"

He stood up, said,

"I don't expect you to understand, but He loves us."

"That's a comfort."

He put out his hand, said,

"No hard feelings."

I ignored his hand, said,

"Cop on."

After he'd gone, I looked at the piece of paper. It had his name

BRENDAN FLOOD

And a phone number.

I was going to sling it but changed my mind.

Went to the florist's. It was the same girl who'd sold me the roses. She said,

"I remember you."

"Right."

"Did they work?"

"What?"

"The roses, for your lady?"

"Good question."

"Ah . . . that's a pity. You're going to try again?"

"Not exactly."

"Oh?"

"I need a wreath."

A look of horror, then,

"Did she die?"

"No . . . no, somebody else, a friend."

"I am sorry."

A small priest walked by. He said,

"How ya."

He had the jolliest face I'd seen in a long time. The girl asked,

"Do you know who that is?"

"He's a small priest."

"He's the bishop."

"You're coddin'!"

"And the loveliest man you'd ever meet."

I was astonished. As a child, I'd known bishops who ruled like feudal lords. That you'd see an exhalted cleric bounce down the street, in relative anonymity, was a revelation.

The girl said if I wrote down the name and details, she'd see to it the wreath was delivered, adding,

"I don't think you want to carry it round town."

I toyed with the notion of bringing the wreath into the bookies but let it go. The girl gave me a measured look, said,

"I'd say you were a fine thing when you were young."

"It's a good year for the roses."

Elvis Costello

Harte's was located off Quay Street. They'd had a bookies shop through three generations. Then the big English firms bought out the local outfits. Harte took the money, then opened right next door. The town was delighted. Not often you got to stick it to the Brits financially.

I'd known Tom Harte a long time. When I entered, he was leaning over form sheets, enveloped in cigarette smoke, said,

"Jack Taylor, by the hokey. Is this a raid?"

"I'm not a guard any more."

"That's what they all say."

"I want to get a bet on."

He extended his arms, encompassing the premises, said,

"You've taken the right turn."

I gave him the name and asked for a price. He checked the teletext, said,

"Thirty-five to one."

I wrote out a docket and laid all my cash beneath. He read it, lowered his voice, asked,

"Are you serious?"

"As the grave."

Two other punters studying the dogs sensed the change in atmosphere, strained to hear. Tom said,

"Jack, I'm a bookie but you're one of our own. There's a hot thing in this race; he'll hack home in a common canter."

212

"All the same."

"I'm trying to do you a favour here."

"Will you take the bet?"

He gave a shrug they perfect in bookie school. I said, "Right, I'll be seeing you."

"Sure you will. Hold that thought."

I checked the docket again and headed out. One of the punters followed, called,

"Jack."

I stopped outside Kenny's, let him catch up. He had the pallor of turf accountant's confinement. The smell of nicotine was massive. The eyes had the mix of fawning and slyness that takes years to achieve. He'd peaked. Gave me the half smile of the damned, asked,

"Got something?"

"Well, I dunno is it any good."

"Come on, Jack, I need a break."

"Rocket Man."

He looked stunned. As if his winning ticket had been disqualified. He said,

"Be serious."

"I am serious."

"Arrah, feck you. What did I expect from a guard?"

Near the Protestant school, just a Catholic away from Victoria Square, is Bailey's Hotel. Now, this is old Galway. New hotels are built on every available space, but Bailey's seems to have escaped the gallop to prosperity. It hasn't been

sold

revamped

rezoned.

In fact, it's rarely noticed.

You don't hear of "commercial travellers" nowadays. But if you'd a mad passion to find one, they'd be at Bailey's. Country people go "for the dinner". The exterior is pure weathered granite and the small sign reads "OTEL". The H is back in the fifties, lost in the mist of Morris Minor aspirations.

On a whim, I went inside. A reception desk is tucked in the corner. An elderly woman was leafing through *Ireland's Own*. I asked,

"Mrs Bailey?"

She looked up and I'd have put her age at eighty. But her eyes were alert. She said,

"Aye."

"I'm Jack Taylor, you knew my father."

It took her a minute and then,

"He worked on the line."

"He did."

"I liked him."

"Me, too."

"Why have you a beard?"

"Notions."

"Foolish notions. Can I help you, young Taylor?"

"I need accommodation . . . long term."

She waved a hand at the décor, said,

"We're not fancy."

"Me either."

"Mm . . . mm . . . there's a bright room on the third floor that's been vacant."

"I'll take it."

"Janet, she cleans every other day, but she sometimes forgets."

"That's fine. Let me pay you."

This was purely a gesture. All my cash was with the bookie. She asked,

"Have you a credit card?"

"No."

"That's good 'cause we don't take them. Pay me the last Friday of the month."

"Thank you. When could I move in?"

"I'll get Janet to air the room and put a kettle in. Anytime after that."

"I really appreciate it, Mrs Bailey."

"Call me Nora. It's just a room, but I hope you'll feel at home."

I already did.

FROM: The Four Agreements
by
Don Miguel Ruiz
NUMBER 2: "*Don't take anything personally.*
Nothing others do is because of you.
It simply reflects their own life
expressions and the training they
received when they were children."

"*. . . dream on.*"

Jack Taylor

That night, I packed. Didn't take long. Punctuated by the six pack. Telling myself,

"Ease on slow with these, maybe I can chill."

Like all lies and the best illusions, it helped me function short time. I lined four black bin bags along the wall, said,

"My wordly possessions I thee endow."

With those

> broken fingers
> a broken nose
> and a beard

I wasn't an advertisement for the Celtic tiger.

The phone went. Picked it up, hoping it was Ann, said,

"Hello."

"Jack, it's Cathy B."

"Oh."

"That's warmth?"

"Sorry, I'm packing."

"A magnum?"

"Gee, that's funny. I'm moving out tomorrow."

"Are you moving in with yer old lady?"

Sign of my age. Thought she meant my mother.

"What?"

"She likes you, Jack. At the gig, she couldn't take her eyes off you."

"Ann! Jesus, no . . . I'm moving into a hotel."

"Weird city, dude. What hotel?"

"Bailey's."

"Never heard of it."

I was glad, meant it was still a Galway thing.

"My friend Sean died."

"The old geezer, who had the pub?"

"Yeah."

"I'm sorry. I think I liked him. Hey, I can get a van, help you move."

"Naw, a cab will handle it."

"OK. Are you free next Friday?"

"Unless they catch me."

"I'm getting married."

"You're kidding . . . to who?"

"Everett, he's a performance artist."

"I'll pretend that makes sense to me. Wow . . . congratulations . . . I think . . . how long have you been dating?"

"Dating! Get with the millennium, Jack. I've been with him . . . like . . . zonks."

I had to allow for her being English and that they'd lost the grip on language, asked,

"How long?"

"It's nearly three weeks."

"Phew, how can you stand the pace?"

"Will you give me away? I mean . . . you're the only old guy I know."

"Thanks . . . sure, I'd be delighted."

Horse time.

Put the TV on, brought up the teletext. Was I nervous? Wiped a light perspiration from my brow. OK

. . . that's the beer. Here we go . . . results . . . scrolled to them. First off, couldn't see it . . . shit . . . maybe he didn't run. Come on . . . come on . . .

ROCKET MAN . . . 12/1

Oh my God.

Won!

Finished at 12's and I'd got 35's. Did a little jig, then punched the air, roared,

"YES!"

Kissed the screen, said,

"Yah little beauty."

Did some fast heart-pounding sums. Seven big ones. Got the docket out, ensured there was no mistake. Nope, it was clear as day. A knock at the door.

I pulled it open. Linda. I said,

"Yeah."

"Jack, I hate to be pushy but I wonder if you'd made any arrangements?"

"I have."

"Oh, that's great. Is it nice?"

"What do you care?"

"I don't want us to part on bad terms."

"Of course. Just 'cause you're evicting me, it shouldn't affect our friendship."

"I feel bad."

I laughed out loud, said,

"That's a tragedy. God forbid you should feel that."

And I shut the door.

All in all, my last evening was one for the books.

"In matters of grave importance
style
not sincerity
is
the vital thing.
Violence requires a cold and deadly style."

Oscar Wilde

Next morning, I was having coffee, checking everything was ready to go. The news was on. I was only half listening till the local news and

A young girl's body was taken from the water at Nimmo's Pier this morning. Gardaí at the scene tried unsuccessfully to revive the girl. This brings to ten, the number of teenage suicides this year from the same spot.

I said,
"He's done it again."
The phone went. It was Ann, no preamble, launched,
"You heard the news."
"Yes."
"You could have prevented it."
And she hung up.
If I had a bottle, I'd have climbed in. Called a cab. I carried my stuff outside and waited by the canal. When I closed the door of the flat, I didn't look back.
The cab driver was a Dub and full of it. I said,
"Bailey's Hotel."
"Where's that?"
I gave him directions and he said,
"How did I miss it?"

I didn't answer. He spent the journey explaining where the GAA were going wrong. I gave appropriate grunts. At the hotel, he gave it the once over, said,

"Jeez, it doesn't look much."

"It's like the GAA . . . you have to be on the inside."

Mrs Bailey was at Reception, asked,

"Need a porter?"

I didn't know if it was a pint or help but shook my head. She added,

"Janet has the room lovely."

She handed me a set of keys, said,

"Come and go as you please."

Beat that.

I'd imagined Janet to be a girl. If anything, she was older than Mrs Bailey. Waiting outside my room, she actually shook my hand, said,

"'Tis great you're from Galway."

The room was bright, spacious, with large windows. A vase of flowers on the table. Janet had followed me in, said,

"Just to welcome you."

A bathroom with a massive tub and acres of fresh clean towels. Beside the double bed was a coffee pot and a pack of Bewley's best. I said,

"You went to a lot of trouble."

"Arrah, not a bit. We haven't had a long-term since Mr Waite passed on."

"How long was he here?"

"Twenty years."

"I'll do the same."

She gave a huge smile. One from the heart. The type that guile or spite has never shadowed. Looking out into the corridor, as if someone might hear, she said,

"We have dances on a Saturday night."

"Really?"

Her face lit up, like a nun with chocolate; she said,

"It's not advertised, not ever. The Swingtime Aces . . . do you know them?"

I didn't, said,

"I do. Great band."

"Oh they're *fabulous*. They do foxtrots and tangos, it's as lively. Do you dance?"

"You should see my rumba."

She near squeaked with delight. I said,

"Save the last dance for me."

I swear, she near skipped off. There was a phone, TV, video. All the essentials. Decided not to unpack. Took the stairs and was on the street in a moment. I wanted a drink so bad, I could taste it on my tongue.

The bookies was empty. Just Harte behind the counter.
Without looking up, he said,
"You've ruined me."
"Didn't you lay it off?"
"Course I did."
"Back it yourself?"
"Course."
"So, how are you hurting?"
"I got blind-sided."
"Don't we all."
"You'll take a cheque?"
"Never happen."
"That's what I thought, here."
Flung a padded envelope on the counter, said,
"You'll want to count it."
I did.
As I was leaving, Harte called,
"Jack!"
"Yeah."
"Don't come back."

*" 'Boy,' Carella said,
'What a day this was!' "*

Ed McBain, *Killer's Wedge*

Walking into Grogan's, I felt the loss of Sean like damnation. The place looked different, was different. The two perennials at the counter weren't there. A large fat man came out of the store room. I asked,

"What happened to the sentries?"

"You wot, guv!"

English.

"Two old guys, propped up the bar like clockwork."

"I got shot of 'em. Bad for business."

"You're Sean's son?"

He gave me a close look, verging on hostility, said,

"Who's asking?"

"I was his friend. Jack Taylor."

Put out my hand. He ignored it, asked,

"Did I meet you at the funeral?"

"I . . . um . . . didn't make it."

"Not much of a friend then, eh."

Nailed me there.

He went behind the counter, began busy bar things. I said,

"Could I get a drink?"

"Naw, I don't think this is your kind of place."

I stood for a moment and he asked,

"Was there something else?"

"I understand now why Sean never mentioned you."

He smirked so I added,

"He must have been ashamed of his life of you."

226

Outside, I felt a mix of rage and sadness, and it's a dangerous cocktail. Wanted to go back and flatten the smug bastard. Two Americans stopped, looked at the pub, asked,

"Is this, like, an authentic pub?"

"No, it's a fake. Go over to Garavan's, it's the real thing."

At the off-licence, I loaded up. The assistant said,

"Bit of a party!"

"Bit of a shambles."

By the time I got back to the hotel, I was feeling the weight. For punishment, I took the stairs. Opened the door of my new room, thought,

"Two seconds to a drink."

The TV was on. I walked in and Sutton was in the armchair, legs propped on the bed. I nearly dropped the booze. He said,

"They show some shit in the mornings."

And he clicked it off.

I tried for composure, asked,

"How did you get in my room?"

"Janet let me in, told her we're brothers. Did you know they have dances here?"

I walked round the chair and he asked,

"What's in the bag, man?"

"How did you know I was here?"

"I've been following you. Make sure you don't get jumped again."

"Following me! Who the fuck do you think you are?"

He stood up, hands out in mock defence, said,

"Ah, you're back."

"Like you didn't know, like you 'forgot' the gin that night."

And realised how that sounded. Whine city. As if it was his fault. Tossed him a can, said,

"Stop following me . . . OK?"

"Okey-dokey."

We drank in silence till he said,

"I went to the funeral."

"More than I did."

"I liked that old bastard. He was a feisty little fuck."

"His son took over the pub."

"Yeah! What's he like?"

"He barred me."

Sutton laughed out loud and I said,

"Thanks a lot."

Not too long till we cracked the seal on the Scotch and he said,

"Planter's done it again."

"Maybe he didn't, maybe it *is* a suicide."

"Come on, Jack. You don't believe that. Right after we confront him, he goes straight out and does a girl. It's 'up yours' to us."

"We can't prove dick."

"So, you're going to let it slide."

"What can I do?"

"You could shoot him."

I looked at Sutton's face. Saw nothing there to indicate he was joking.

Next morning, I was frayed but not wiped. I'd gone to bed the previous lunchtime and, miraculously, stayed there. I was hurting but it was manageable. Hunched over coffee, I was muttering. A knock at the door. Janet. She said,

"Oh, sorry, I can come back later."

"Just give me ten, I'm outa here."

She stood at the door and I snapped,

"Was there something?"

"Your brother, I hope I did the right thing."

"That's OK."

"He's a lovely man, promised me a painting."

"That's him all right."

"Well, I'll leave you in peace."

I counted my winnings. Spread the cash on the bed and marvelled. Then I got some envelopes and put a wedge in for the guy who gave me the tip. Next, a wedge for Padraig, the head wino. An envelope for Cathy B.'s wedding present, and that was it.

Time to visit Sean. There was a bus I could get but felt I'd try to walk through the hangover. It's a hike. From Eyre Square to Woodquay, out by the Dyke Road, on to the Quincenntenial Bridge. Up and on to Rahoon. I remember the old gates of the cemetery. Gone now. A photo of them, by Ann Kennedy, hung in Kenny's with lines from Joyce's poem.

My legs were aching in rhythm with my head. I had no intention of visiting my father. Truth was, I felt ashamed. My endeavours of the past weeks were nothing I wanted to bring to him.

Found Sean's grave without trouble. It was alight with flowers. The temporary marker was the song of forlorn. If I had a cap, I'd have taken it off.

Blessed myself. Some rituals just surface without beckoning, I said,

"Sean, I miss you terrible. I didn't value the worth of you.

"I'm drinking again and that's sure to piss you off. I'm sorry I was that very worst of things, a poor friend. I have no pub now either. I'll come and see you lots. Your son's an asshole."

I might have cried had I been able. As I walked away, I glanced in my father's direction. A woman was kneeling there. For one wild glorious moment, I thought it was Ann. The sheer exhilarating joy.

My mother. Her head down, reciting the rosary. I gave a small cough. She looked up, said,

"Jack."

I put out my hand to help her up. Couldn't help but notice how frail she was. The knuckles on her hand, swollen from arthritis. She was, of course, in the regulation black. I said,

"I didn't know you came."

"There's a lot you don't know, Jack."

"I don't doubt it."

She looked at the grave, then asked,

"Could we go for a cup of tea?"

"Um . . ."

"I'll pay. We could get a taxi, too. Go to the GBC . . . they've lovely buns."

I shook my head. She added,

"I put a bouquet on Sean's grave. You'll miss him."

"I'll manage."

"I'll get a mass for him. At the Augustinian. It's only a pound there."

I nearly said,

"That's right, get the best rate, yah cheap bitch."

But bit down. She said,

"He liked that church, went to mass there every morning."

"Look, I . . . have to go."

Maybe she said, "Bye, Jack," but I didn't hear it. Could feel her eyes as I walked away. Passing through the gates I thought,

"Both my parents are here now."

The leavings of
an inarticulate thanks.

The next few days, I exerted massive control and kept my drinking to a level. A level of wanting. Wanting gallons more.

But I was doing two pints at lunch, then holding out till late evening when I'd slow chug two more pints with Jameson chasers.

I knew how fragile this balance was. A gust of wind would plunge me back to hell. The buzz was sufficient to keep me that beat outside reality and I clung fast.

I'd met my tipster and given him his envelope. He was surprised, said,

"Jaysus, I'm surprised."

"Well, you gave me the information. It's the least I could do. Did you back it yourself?"

"Back what?"

"Rocket Man! The tip you gave me."

"Naw, I never do tips."

I felt he'd have been a whizz in the post office. No sign of Padraig, and I'd checked his haunts.

I rang Ann, felt if I could just see her, we might have a shot. As soon as she heard my voice, she hung up. My beard was full arrived, complete with grey flashes. Told myself it spoke of character, even maturity. Odd times I caught my reflection, I saw the face of desperation.

My plan, as I said at the beginning, was to go to London, get a place by the park and wait. Now I had the money and a reason to wait. Began to scan the English papers for accommodation.

The only thing holding me was a resolution to Sarah's death. I was in no doubt that Planter was responsible. I hadn't a clue how to prove it, but I couldn't leave without some answer.

Found a new pub. Over my years as a garda and after, I'd been barred from every pub in the city. Now though, along with prosperity came new pubs. Tried a few truly horrendous ones. You went in and a babe greeted you with a total welcome.

The

"AND HOW ARE YOU TODAY?"

You half expected to be asked your star sign. Walking into one of these places with a high scale hangover, the last item you wanted was enthusiasm. Hangovers can only deal with surliness.

I found Nestor's by accident. I was walking down Forster Street when the downpour came. The type of rain that *is* personal. You're instantly drenched. Stepped into a side street and there it was. Knew I was in business as a sign on the window proclaimed:

WE DO NOT STOCK BUD LIGHT

Went in and couldn't believe it, one of the sentries was propped. He nodded, asked,

"What kept you?"

"Where's the other guy?"

"He had a heart attack."

"Jaysus, how is he?"

"If you had one, how'd you be?"

"Right. Can I get you a jar?"

He looked at me as if I'd propositioned him, asked,

"Will I have to buy you one back?"

"No."

"And you won't put chat on me?"

"Count on it."

"All right then."

The pub was old, like a small kitchen. Could hold twenty customers tops. The barman was in his fifties. Two professions that require age

> Barmen
>
> and
>
> Barbers

He didn't know me. What a bonus. I ordered the drink and looked round. Those old signs for Guinness, a guy lifting a wagon and two dray horses with the immortal words:

GUINNESS IS GOOD FOR YOU

Authentic, right down to rust. My own favourite is the pelican with a feast of creamy pints in his beak. Now, that is one happy bird. There were signs for Woodbines and Sweet Afton. Even had the lines from Robbie Burns. The barman said,

"I don't like change."

"Gets my vote."

"Guy was in the other day, wanted to buy the signs."

236

"Everything's for sale."

"Not here it isn't."

I went and grabbed a corner. Wooden table, old hardback chair. The door opened, a large farmer came in, said to no one in particular,

"We'll hardly get a summer."

My kinda place.

OF

THE

WINO

Mrs Bailey said,

"You've got mail!"

"What!"

She handed me a letter. I didn't know how it could be possible. Opened it:

THE DEPARTMENT OF JUSTICE

A Chara,

In compliance with the terms of your termination, it is required you surrender all property belonging to the Government.

See Article 59347A of Uniform and Equipment. It has come to our attention you have failed to return Item 8234 — A regulation garda all-weather coat.

We trust in your speedy return of said item.

I bundled it up. Mrs Bailey asked,

"Bad news?"

"Same old."

"I've noticed, Mr Taylor, you don't take breakfast."

"Call me Jack. No, I'm not big on mornings."

She gave a small smile. I knew she'd never call me Jack. As certain as Item 8234 not being speedily returned. She said,

"I haven't had breakfast since the fourth of August, 1984."

"Oh."

"That was the day my husband died, Lord rest him."

"I see."

I didn't. But what the hell. She continued,

"I had a big breakfast that day. It was after the races and we'd been busy. Oh my, we had the business of the town back then. I remember it so clearly. I had

2 Rashers

Black Pudding

2 Sausages

Fried Bread

And two cups of tea. Then I read the *Irish Independent*."

She gave a nervous laugh.

"Whoops. Now you know my politics. Anyway, I went up to call Tom. He was dead. Him lying cold and me stuffing myself."

I didn't have a clue as to how to respond. Sometimes, though, when people reveal a piece, they don't want an answer, just a receiver. Then she said,

"I miss the sausages. From McCambridge's. They have them made special."

Now she composed herself, got her hotel face in place, said,

"I wonder if I might have a few minutes of your time? Something I'd like your views on."

"Sure, whenever you like."

"Grand. I'll be closing the bar round eleven. We could have a nightcap."

Bar! Jesus, right under my nose.

Go figure.

240

I said,
"I'll look forward to it."
"God bless, Mr Taylor."

Outside, considered my options. I wanted to find Padraig. The envelope for him was burning a hole in my pocket. With my brown envelopes, I felt like a little government.

Went to Nestor's. The sentry was in place but I ignored him. I could feel his gratitude. The bar guy nodded and I said,

"You do coffee?"

He held up a mug, said,

"Sure do."

Took the hard chair. The daily papers were spread on the table. Took the *Independent*. For Mrs Bailey, if no other reason.

Top story was about a man who'd had his new car stolen. He lived in a neighbourhood with a heavy influx of refugees. Later the same day, a Romanian had asked him for money. The man had beaten him to an inch of his life. It turned out a local kid had "borrowed" the car.

My coffee arrived and the bar guy said,

"He lost his car, but the other poor bastard lost his country."

I put the paper down. He said,

"The new Ireland. Ten years from now, I'll be serving Romanian-Irish, African-Irish."

Thought I'd best play my cards, said,

"Better than the parish pump shite of the fifties."

"Way better."

On Eyre Square, I approached a band of winos. Most were semi-conscious, nodding to the phantom orchestra. I'd heard some of the music in my time. I asked,

"Anyone seen Padraig?"

A guy with a Boyzone sweatshirt and a Glasgow accent said,

"Wit di ya win wit im, Jimmy?"

Roughly translated means,

"Why?"

"I'm a friend of his."

He conferred with his colleagues. A woman rose from the group. She gave new dimensions to the description "bedraggled", croaked,

"He's in hospital."

"What happened."

"The Salthill bus hit him."

The way she put it, sounded like the bus had been gunning for him. The Glasgow guy asked,

"Pris i cip i tee, Jimmy?"

I handed over some cash. This brought a shower of blessings, benedictions and spittle. God knows, I needed them.

Only later did it register that the woman had an American accent. The drinking school had gone international. A United Nations of Despair. I checked an old copy of Ross McDonald and found this nugget.

There were drab thumbprints under her eyes. Maybe she had been up all night. Americans never grow old, they died: and her eyes had guilty knowledge of it.

I headed for the hospital. Foreboding writ large.

So that's the list
I said at last
so full of breeze, so full of
booze,
well let me sign it with
a flourish, end it with
a sadder kiss
just one of course.

En route to the hospital, I bought

> Roll-up tobacco
> Paper
> 3 Pairs of thermal socks.

I made enquiries from a porter. He was obstructive as required by his status. Eventually I got through to him. Cash helped. He said,

"The oul wino. He's in St Joseph's Ward. He's had his final blast of meths."

"Thank you for sharing."

"What?"

I didn't recognise Padraig, not only because they'd washed him, but he'd shrunk.

"How yah?" I said.

"They won't let me smoke."

"Bad bastards. Will I roll you one?"

"I would be for ever in your debt. They are not overly fond of me here. Do my brethren on the square prosper?"

"They were all asking for you."

They'd already forgotten him. He knew that. Gave a tight smile. I lit the rollie and put it in his mouth. Coughs and chest rumbles danced him in the bed. He said,

"I needed that. Did I ever acquire your name?"

"Jack."

246

"Suits you. That it's also the name of my favourite beverage is the sharp side of irony. Lying here, nicotineless and gasping for a drink, I pondered God. I think I heard once that He knew my name before I was born. Have you any thoughts on that?"

I took a furtive look round the ward. People were pointedly ignoring us. The word was out on the wino. He began to shiver. The heat was on full throttle. I could feel sweat in my beard. A tea trolley came, pushed by a middle-aged knacker called Rooney.

A small spit of a man who put the taste into venom. My father, the most peaceful of men, was rumoured to have given him a hiding. He distributed tea and dead biscuits to all except Padraig.

"Hey, hey, Rooney," I shouted.

He pretended not to hear me and the trolley accelerated as he reached the corridor.

Cold.

The cold flash of a killing rage.

Blind.

I caught him near the Coronary Unit. The darting eyes threw the challenge to me. His catering badge "Mr Rooney" gave him status. The look said,

"You can't touch me!"

I'm over six foot, weigh in at 180 lbs. I felt like two of myself. My voice came gut low.

"Do you get to Casualty?"

"No, I don't, I go to . . ."

And he launched into a litany of saints. Representing the various wards. I said,

247

"You're going to be in Casualty in about five minutes because I'm going to break your left arm!"

"What's the matter with you, Taylor? I never did nothing to you. I was a great pal of your oul fellah's."

"Go back up that corridor. Wheel your bag of tricks into the ward and *offer* that man a cup of tea . . . oh, and one of them mouldy biscuits."

He raised up on his toes, asked,

"Arrah, a wino . . . what do you care . . . what's he to you? 'Tisn't tea the likes of him wants."

As he finished, I stared into his eyes. Let him see what even I don't acknowledge. He turned the trolley round and served Padraig his afternoon tea . . . and *two* biscuits. I even had a cup myself, declined seconds.

After, Padraig said,

"I won't make the square for the races."

"You might."

"No. I'd have liked to wear them new socks. Do you think . . . do you think you could fit them on me now. I'm perished."

He surely was.

The socks were red thermal. Said on the front . . . "Cosy Fit". That near did me in.

I rolled back the blanket and his feet were a sin. A serious novelist would call them

> gnarled
> twisted
> lacerated
> and oh
> so very old.

The socks were a size medium and enormous on him. He watched me watching them. I asked,

"How's that?"

"Mighty, I'm the better of them already. I had a pair of Argylls once, or maybe I just hope I did. You have a rare gift, my friend."

"Do I?"

"You never probe or pry into a person's affairs."

"Thank you."

Not much of a recommendation for an investigator. It was time to leave. I said,

"I'll bring you a drop of the creature."

He gave a lovely smile, said,

"Any creature."

Then leant out of the bed, rummaged in a locker and brought out some battered sheets of paper, said,

"Read this, my friend, but not now. You'll know the time."

"That's a bit mysterious."

"Without mystery, we are lost!"

Question: *"What do you know about money?"*
Young Man: *"Not a lot."*
Answer: *"It's how they keep score."*

Bill James, *Gospel*

Outside the hospital, the black dog descended. A cloud of depression that begged, "End it now."

Used to be, the best early house was right opposite the hospital. Gone, of course. Now you have The River Inn. I chanced it. Not a sign of the river.

A young woman tending bar, complete with name tag:

SHONA

Jeez, for the days of Mary.

She gave me a smile full of capped teeth. I hated her, said,

"Jameson and water."

Figured she couldn't screw that up. She didn't.

Though she did add ice. Worse, she hovered. I said,

"Don't you have to floss or something?"

Took a window seat and realised I'd forgotten to give Padraig his money. A middle-aged woman was going table to table distributing leaflets. Dropped one hastily on mine, without eye contact. No doubt Shona had clued her in. I read:

Till now, they and their ancestors have been in revolt against me. The sons are defiant and obstinate . . .

That was enough.

I focused on a phone in the corner and had to suppress a wild ache to call Ann. Bit hard on the ice and waited for the impulse to leak away. A mantra unreeled in my head, like this:

I have money, lots of money. As long as I have that, I'm
   in the game.
Never-no-mind I can't figure the game. Cash says I'm in.

Over and over till the ice melted in the glass.

When I arrived at the hospital that evening, I had a bottle of Jack Daniels for Padraig. His bed was empty. I grabbed a passing nurse, asked,

"Is he gone?"

"I'm afraid so. At 4.30, very peacefully."

"What?"

"He didn't suffer."

"You mean he's dead!"

"I'm afraid so . . . are you a relative?"

I tried to get my mind in gear, asked,

"What happens to him now?"

She explained that if no one "claimed" him, the Western Health Board would do the burial. I said,

"A pauper's grave?"

"Well, we don't term it that any more. There are spaces reserved in the cemetery."

"I'll claim him."

In a daze, I went through the rigmarole of forms and certificates. Even rang an undertaker's who said they'd handle everything. I asked,

"Do you take cash?"

"We do."

Padraig's funeral, the burial, I can only vaguely recall. I was there at every stage but pumped to the eyeballs. Course, there were no mourners. I got this gig all to myself.

Here's the thing. He's buried close to Sean. I couldn't have planned it better. I think Sutton might have showed during some of the proceedings, but perhaps that's wishful thinking.

Ann certainly didn't.

When it was done, I had to apologise to Mrs Bailey for missing our nightcap. She gave me the strangest look, said,

"But we *had* our nightcap."

Total blank. Trying to cover, I said,

"I meant I wasn't much help."

"But you were a tremendous help."

"I was?"

"Certainly. After your impassioned plea, how could I possibly sell."

Some mysteries are best left alone. Padraig had that right. Finally, I got round to looking at the papers he'd given me.

This is what he'd written:

An Irish Wino Foresees His Death
(with apologies to W.B.)

Blame it on an intuition
I hadn't acted
and certainly

would nigh on certainty
believe
a life upon the streets
at least for long
I'd not survive.
The sabotage
of hope
for far too long
I'd lived
one drink above despair
a public house
a hearse
before
I watched a wino
place his hand
above his heart.

I'd known
a cap
if he had owned
would slow and
very slow
remove
shake so
the shakes . . . disregarding
. . . a Silence in Respect.

The cortège pass . . . press on . . . to press
his hand . . . the day across
this moment new
passed nigh beyond

the oldest expectation
a hand towards
reconciliation . . . not renewed.

The coffin doesn't pass
the rich hotels
their hands
towards the meth remains
aren't shaped.

BREAK POINT

Things broke very quickly after that. I can't say Padraig's death was a turning point, but it appears so. A night in Nestor's, the barman took me aside, said,

"No lectures right, but I used to drink like you do. Which is fine, but I think you have unfinished business."

"What are you on about?"

"You have the face of a man who needs to be elsewhere. So, here."

He handed me a packet. I was at my most belligerent, growled,

"What the hell is this?"

"Beta blockers. Chill you right down. Like cocaine without the damage."

"What makes you think I . . ."

But he shu . . . sh . . . ed me, said,

"Try these . . . chill . . . and when you've finished whatever the hell's haunting you, come back . . . settle into a sedate life of the newspapers, a few pints and a decent pub."

Then he was gone. I said,

"You need help, you do."

Put the packet in my pocket all the same.

Wouldn't you know, next morning, I'd the mother of a hangover. Took one of the tablets in desperation. A little while, I was becalmed.

Looking out the window, or rather, looking calmly out, I said,

"This doesn't mean I'll stop drinking."

But it did.

Cathy B.'s wedding should have been a massive piss-up. It was, but not for me. The Registrar is in Mervue, opposite Merlin Park Hospital. I said to Cathy,

"Wouldn't you have liked a church?"

"Negative waves, Jack."

Her intended, Everett, the performance artist, wasn't as bad as I feared. Bad enough but tolerable. Early twenties with the shaved skull. He was wearing what I think they call a kaftan . . . or curtains. To be fair, it appeared to be fresh ironed. For the occasion, I guess. Cathy looked gorgeous. In a simple red dress and killer heels. She asked,

"Wotcha fink?"

"Lady in Red."

Mega smile. When she introduced me to Everett, he said,

"Ah . . . the old guy."

I tried to act as if I cared, asked him,

"How's . . . the . . . performing?"

"I'm resting."

"Right."

That was our talk over. God knows, I've met bigger assholes. He was simply the youngest. Cathy whispered,

"He's very modest. He's got a big gig soon with Macnas."

"OK."

I handed her the envelope. She shrieked,
"How *Godfather II*."
The ceremony was

> brief
> precise
> cold.

You need a church.

Reception after in The Roisín. Barrels of drink rolled out. It was packed with arts people. The ones who can tell at fifty yards you're non-art. Pretty good band though. Playing bluegrass through punk-country to salsa. Got that crowd hopping. A young woman in black denim asked me,
"Wanna dance?"
"Maybe later."
She gave me an ice appraisal, said,
"I don't think you got a later."
I blamed the beard. A few times I hovered near the bar, near shouted,
"Double Jameson and a pint."
But passed. Cathy asked,
"You don't wanna drink?"
"Oh I do . . . but . . ."
"Gotcha. You're nicer without it."
When I was leaving she gave me a huge hug, said,
"You're cool."
Everett gave me a slow nod, said,
"Hang tough, dude."
Words, no doubt, to live by.

Saw the headline as I walked up Dominick Street:

TOP BUSINESSMAN DISAPPEARS
SOUGHT IN TEENAGE SUICIDES PROBE

I bought the paper, sat on the bridge to read. The gist of the article was as follows:

A former garda, Brendan Flood, has come forward to allege that Mr Planter, a prominent businessman, is linked to the deaths of a number of teenage girls. Their deaths had been classified as suicide, but in light of Mr Flood's revelations, their cases are being reopened.

Superintendent Clancy, in a brief statement, said Mr Planter had disappeared from his home and his whereabouts are unknown.

Mr Flood said he'd decided to come forward because of his recent embracing of Christian beliefs.

Another ex-garda, Jack Taylor, was mentioned by Mr Flood as "being instrumental" in his decision to come forward.

I put the paper down, thought, "Fame at last."

Gave a sigh of something close to relief. So, it was nearly over. Ann was getting what she so desperately required. That the world would know her daughter was not a suicide. Reading the piece, you'd think I'd been a player. Truth to tell, I'd fumbled and fecked, made waves without caution and caused the death of Ford.

I slung the paper.

Back in my room, the thirst was on me. The voice whispering,

"Case closed, mostly solved, time for R and R." Took my beta-b and went to bed.

"Clay stood there for a few more minutes, just shaking his head, thinking how funny it was. Once you fuck up, seems you can't STOP fucking up to save your life."

George P. Pelecanos, *The Sweet Forever*

Next morning, early, there was a knock at my door. Expecting Janet, I said,

"Come in."

It was Sutton. He said,

"What have you got to drink?"

"Coffee."

"Ah shit, you're on the wagon again."

"What can I tell you?"

He sat in the armchair, got his legs up on the bed. I said,

"You've heard about Planter?"

"Sure. I can go one better."

"How do you mean?"

"I know where he is."

"You're kidding. Did you tell the guards?"

"You were a guard, I'm telling you."

I reached for the phone and he said,

"It's not that kind of gig."

"I don't understand you."

"I can bring you to see him."

Took me a moment, then I said,

"You *took* him!"

He gave that smile, asked,

"You want to meet him or not?"

I figured it was the only deal, then said,

"OK."

He leaped to his feet, said,

264

"Let's rock 'n' roll."

It was the yellow car again. He said,

"The colour grows on you."

After half an hour, I said,

"Clifden? . . . you've got him in Clifden!"

"I told you I got that warehouse. Huge place. I offered you to share."

"So . . . you kidnapped a lodger, that it?"

Part of me thought it was some crazy joke, but I had to check it out, asked,

"What are you doing with him?"

"Painting his portrait. He commissioned me, remember?"

Naturally, it was raining when we got to Clifden. About halfway down the Sky Road, he stopped, pulled into a layby, said,

"It's uphill now."

I looked but couldn't see a house. He said,

"That's the beauty, you can't see it from the road."

Got drenched going up, slipped twice in the mud. Came over a rise and there it was. Sutton said,

"He'll be glad of the company."

The building was painted a drab green, blended perfectly. A series of windows were shuttered close. Sutton produced a key, opened the door, shouted,

"I'm home, dear."

He stepped inside, then shouted,

"Aw fuck!"

I brushed past him. In the half light I could see a bunk bed. A figure hanging above it. Sutton hit the light.

Planter was hanging from a wooden beam, a sheet around his neck. A leg iron, attached to his ankle, was bolted near the bed. I glanced quickly at his face, and Christ, he had suffered.

A painter's easel was near the bed, a canvas in preparation. Sutton said,

"The fuck took the easy way out."

I looked again at Planter's face, said,

"You call that easy . . . Jesus!"

Sutton moved to a cupboard, took out a bottle of Scotch, asked,

"Hit yah?"

I shook my head. He took a large gulp, gasped,

"Whoo . . . that helps."

I walked over to Sutton, asked,

"Did you kill him?"

The whisky had already reached his eyes, giving them a wild cast. He said,

"Are you fucking mad, what do you think I am?"

I didn't answer that. He drank more and I asked,

"What now?"

"Let's dump him off Nimmo's, poetic justice."

"I don't think so."

"Then we'll have to bury the prick."

That's what we did. Behind the house. The rain was savage and digging that hard ground took over two hours.

Finally, it was done and I asked,

"Should we say something over him."

"Yeah, something artistic, him liking paintings."

"Any thoughts?"

"Hung in Clifden."

It was six in the evening by the time we got back to Galway. I was wet, dirty, and bone weary. When Sutton parked the car, he said,

"Don't sweat it. He confessed, you know. Gave the girls Rohypnol."

"Why did he drown them?"

"For kicks."

"God almighty."

He seemed to be weighing something, and I said,

"What?"

"He told me about the girls. I mean, he seemed to *want* to tell. But . . ."

"But what?"

"He said the Henderson girl . . . you know . . . Sarah . . ."

"What about her?"

"He didn't kill her — she killed herself."

"The lying fuck."

"Why would he lie? I mean, he admitted the others."

I started to get out of the car, said,

"Listen . . . I don't think I want to see you for a bit."

"Gotcha."

He burned rubber out of there.

When the dust settles
you're left
with dust.

The search for Planter occupied the headlines for a while. After a few weeks, it tapered off and he joined Shergar, Lord Lucan, in speculative space. Cathy B. went off on honeymoon to Kerry and was gone for a month. I heard nothing from Ann.

I didn't drink.

Sutton rang me once. Like that.

"Jack . . . hey, buddy, how yah doing?"

"OK."

"It's OK to ring you though, isn't it? . . . I mean, we have some history now . . . eh?"

"If you say so."

"I hear you're still teetotal."

"You hear right."

"You ever want to cut loose, you know who to call."

"Sure."

"So, Jack, don't you want to hear how I'm doing?"

"If you want to tell me."

Can you give an audible smirk. Sure sounded like that. He said,

"Man, I've been painting, it's what I do."

"Right."

"All right, Jack, don't be a stranger."

Clicked off.

AUTOPSY

Body of a white male
Mid 50's
Tattoo of an angel on right shoulder
Well nourished
Weight: 180 lbs
Height: 6'2"
Cause of death: Ennui

I figured that's how it would be. I could see my naked white flabby torso on the metal tray.

Even hear the dry, detached tone of the medical examiner.

They're the sort of thoughts I was having.

Time to go.

I still had a fair whack of cash. Went into a travel agency.
A middle-aged woman with the name tag "JOAN", said,
"I know you."
"You do?"
"You were courting Ann Henderson."
"The operative word is *were*."
She tut-tutted. It's a bizarre sound. She said,
"That's a crying shame. She's a grand girl."
"I wonder could we do some travel stuff?"
She didn't like it, said,
"Well, *excuse* me. How may I help?"
"A ticket to London."
"Departure date."
"About ten days."
"The return will cost you . . . let's see."
"Joan . . . yo . . . I want a single."
She looked up sharply, asked,
"You're not coming back?"
I gave her my dead smile. She said,
"Suit yourself."
A few minutes later, I had the ticket. I asked,
"Take cash?"
She did, if reluctantly. As I left I said,
"I'll miss you, Joan."
Crossing the square, I swear I saw Padraig near the
fountain. Asked myself, "Is this sobriety all it's cracked
up to be?"

Went to Nestor's. The sentry was there and spoke.

"I read about you in the papers."

"Ah, that was ages ago."

The barman smiled. I since learned his name was Jeff. Despite my daily visits, I'd found out nothing else. I'd estimated he was in my age range. The similar aura of bewilderment and battering surrounded him. I thought that explained the easiness I felt in his company.

I took my hard chair and he brought me coffee, asked,

"Mind if I join you?"

I was amazed. Our relationship seemed to have been solidified on friendly avoidance. I said,

"Sure."

"How are the betas going?"

"I'm not drinking."

He nodded, seemed to weigh up some possibilities, then,

"Do you want me to tell you the truth or will I just play you along?"

"What?"

"That's a Tom Waits' quote."

"No stranger to a bevy himself."

He ran his hands through his hair, said,

"I don't do friends very good. Not that I'm hurting. My wife left me 'cause she said I was too self-sufficient."

I had no idea where this was going. But I'm Irish, I know how this works. The verbal tit-for-tat. You get a personal detail, you fire one back. Piece by piece. A friendship evolves — or not.

A tapestry of talk.

I opened with,

"I don't have a lot of luck with friends. Two of my best are recently buried. I don't know what they got from me except a couple of cheap wreaths on their graves. That and a pair of thermal socks."

He nodded, said,

"Lemme get the coffee pot."

He did.

Recaffeinated, he said,

"I know a bit about you. Not that I asked. But I'm a barman, I hear stuff. I know you helped break that suicide business. How you used to be a guard. Word is, you're a hard case."

I gave a rueful laugh and he continued.

"Me ... I used to be in a band. Ever heard of 'Metal'?"

"Heavy Metal?"

"That too, but 'Metal' was the band. We were big in Germany, late seventies. Anyway, that's how I bought the pub."

"Do you still play?"

"God, no. I didn't play then either. I wrote the lyrics. And need I tell you, lyrics are not vital for head banging. I have two passions, poetry and bikes."

"I think that's logical in a convoluted fashion."

"Not any bikes. Just the Harley. Mine is a softail custom."

I nodded as if this meant a lot. It meant zilch. He continued,

"Thing is, they're a bastard to get parts for. And like any thoroughbred, they break down a lot."

Any more nodding, I'd have a habit.

He was on his feet now. Truth to tell, I envied his enthusiasm. To have such passion. He said,

"Now poetry. It doesn't break down. Upstairs I have the giants . . . know who?"

What the hell, I could play safe, said,

"Yeats
Wordsworth."

He was shaking his head, said,

"Rilke
Lowell
Baudelaire
MacNeice."

Now he looked right at me, said,

"There is a point to all this, and God knows, I'll finally make it."

Handed me a batch of papers, said,

"There are poets among us. These are by people here in Galway. The Fred Johnston one . . . well, I thought it would help with the deaths you've experienced."

"Thanks a lot."

"Don't read them now. Grab a quiet moment, see how they read."

Then he was off doing bar stuff. The sentry said,

"I read about you in the paper."

I could only hope this wasn't going to become a mantra with him.

"He could say it wasn't fair but he'd already said it a million times in his life. In spite of its truth, the idea counted far less than it should."

T. Jefferson Parker, *The Blue Hour*

We hit on a week of glorious weather. Sun from morning till late evening. The city went mad. Work was abandoned and crowds were out getting them rays. Any fear of skin cancer was completely ignored.

Ice cream vendors on every corner. Lager louts in loud array. Worse, men in shorts! With socks and sandals. One of the true horrible sights of the new era.

I don't do sun.

I'm delighted with the lack of rain and anything over is over-indulgence. I don't trust it. Makes you yearn. For things that cannot last.

I was sitting in the shade at Eyre Square. Watching girls, already red, going for blisters. Heard my name . . . saw Fr Malachy. In civvies, chinos and a white t-shirt. I asked,

"Day off?"

"Isn't this heat fierce?"

Course, fierce is the double-edged. Either fierce good or fierce bad. You don't ever ask. You're supposed to know.

I didn't ask. He said,

"You're a hard fellah to find."

"Depends who's looking."

"I was on the beach yesterday. Cripes, it was packed. Had a lovely swim. Do you know who I saw?"

"Malachy, I can safely say I haven't a notion."

"Your friend . . . Sutton."

"Yeah?"

"Surly fellah."

"He doesn't like priests."

"Well, he's a Northerner! I stopped to say hello, asked him if he had a dip?"

I laughed in spite of myself. Malachy continued,

"He told me he can't swim, can you credit that?"

A woman passed, said,

"God bless you, Father."

He said,

"I'll have to go, I'm due on the links in an hour."

"Gee, the Lord is pretty demanding."

He gave me the ecclesiastical look, said,

"You never had a bit of reverence, Jack."

"Oh, I do. I just don't revere the things you do."

Then he was gone. Probably a trick of the light, but the shade seemed to have receded.

On the road leading to Rahoon Cemetery is a new hotel. Jeez, talk about strategic planning. I was tempted to check it out but kept going.

The heat was ferocious. Story of my life, the hordes head for the beach, I'm going to the graveyard. Sunshine bounced off the headstones like calculated revenge. I knelt at Sean's and said,

"I'm not drinking . . . OK?"

Then I went to Padraig, said,

"I didn't bring flowers. I did bring a poem. Which says, even if I'm a cheap bastard, I'm a cheap *artistic* bastard. And God knows, you loved words. Here it is,

COUNTRY FUNERAL

They hold the sea on their right hand
Swaying uphill in a light memorial breeze
The fields here are all rock and bog
And dead trees.

The church sits whitefaced in a wet sun
The islands under the stare of her dark door
Small prayers ascend into a low, cold sky,
Earthed no more.

The hearse engine's out of tune, black
Paint peels to a rust of raw skin, its chrome

Is leafing. Everything comes to its season,
The dead go home.

Perspiration was pouring from me. I began to walk
down the path between the graves. Saw Ann Henderson
coming down the opposite side. We'd meet at the gate.
I considered back-stepping, but she spotted me and
waved.

When I drew level she was smiling. My heart began
to beat with insane hope. I let myself feel how much I'd
missed her. She said,

"Jack!"

I, originally enough, said,

"Ann."

Dragged my mind into gear, asked,

"Want to get a mineral?"

"I'd love to."

We walked down to the hotel, her saying,

"Isn't the heat fierce?"

And how relieved she was at Sarah not being labelled
a suicide.

I said precious little. So afraid was I of blowing the
slim chance I felt on offer. At the hotel, we ordered
large orange crush, tons of ice. She didn't comment on
my non-alcoholic choice. Before I could get into any
kind of appeal, she said,

"Jack, I have wonderful news."

"Yeah?"

"I've met a fantastic man."

I know she talked on but I didn't hear any more.
Finally, we got up to leave and she said,

"I'm going to call a cab, can I drop you?"

I shook my head. For one awful moment I thought she was going to shake my hand. Instead, she leant over and pecked my cheek.

As I walked down towards Newcastle, the sun hammered me. I held my face up, said,

"Roast me, yah bastard."

GOING
MOBILE

Back at my room, I felt gutted. Wanted to drink so ferociously I could taste whisky in my mouth. My heart was a dead thing in my chest. Aloud I shouted Irish of my childhood,

"*An bronach mhor.*"

It's along the lines of, woe is me, but a more contemporary translation might be,

"I'm fucked."

Was I ever.

Circling fifty years of age, was I going to get another shot at love?

Dream on.

Out of left field came a thought:

"Wouldn't it be something to leave Galway sober."

That got me up and swallowing a beta-b, murmuring,

"I've things to do, I gotta prepare for departure."

Nick Hornby had popularised lists. Well I could do an exit one.

Pack

> 3 White Shirts
> 3 jeans
> 1 suit
> some books
> two videos

Then said,

"Screw the suit."

I could carry most in a shoulder bag and be history. Checked my flight ticket, five days to go. Went down to reception, the beta already chilling my soul.

Mrs Bailey asked,

"Mr Taylor, are you OK?"

"Sure."

"Your eyes, they look devastated."

"Aw no, I got shampoo in them."

We let that lie fly for a moment.

I said,

"Mrs Bailey, I'm going to be away for a while."

She didn't seem surprised, said,

"I'll keep your room for you."

"Well, it might be quite a while."

"Don't worry, there'll be *some* room."

"Thank you."

"I liked having you here, you're a good man."

"Oh, I don't know about that."

"Course you don't, that's part of your goodness."

"Could I buy you a nightcap before I leave?"

"Young man, I insist on it."

A yellow car was parked outside. Above the number plate was a "CLFD" sticker. I rapped on the window. Sutton said,

" 'Tis yourself."

"I thought we agreed you'd stop following me."

"I'm not following, I'm waiting."

"What's the difference?"

"You're the detective."

He got out and stretched, said,

"These surveillance gigs are a bastard!"

He was dressed completely in black. Sweat, combat trousers, Nikes. I asked,

"What's with the gear?"

"I'm in mourning."

"I'm not sure that's in the best of taste."

He reached into the car, took out a holdall, said,

"I come bearing gifts."

"Why?"

"I sold another painting; come on, I'll buy you a drink . . . whoops . . . a coffee . . . and shower you with largesse."

I decided it would probably be the last time.

We went to Elles on Shop Street. Sutton said,

"They do great cappuccino."

They did.

Even put an Italian chocolate on the side. Sutton bit into his, said,

"Mm . . . good."

"Have mine."

"You sure, 'cause these are like . . . wicked."

He reached into the holdall, took out two mobile phones, placed one before me, said,

"One for you."

And placed the second before him. I said,

"I don't want one."

"Course you do. I got them cheap. Now we're truly connected. I took the liberty of putting my number in your menu."

Into the bag again and out comes a small, framed painting. Nimmo's Pier. He said,

"You don't have to tell me it's good, I already know that. What it is . . . is valuable. I'm collectable."

I wasn't sure how to proceed so went direct, said,

"I'm leaving."

"Jesus, at least finish the cappuccino."

"No, I'm leaving Galway."

He seemed truly astonished, asked,

"To go where?"

"London."

"That shit hole. I mean, you're not even drinking. How could you go there sober?"

"Lots do . . . apparently."

"Sure, citizens and ghost people. What will you do?"

"Rent a place in Bayswater, hang out."

"Hang yerself. I give you a week."

"Thanks for the vote of confidence."

"Aw . . . London . . . for Chrissakes. When?"

"About five days."

"Are we going to have a farewell drink or what?"

"Sure."

And I indicated the mobile, added,

"I can call you."

"Do. Nights are best. I don't sleep so good."

"No?"

"Would you . . . with a guy buried outside the window?"

I stood up, said,

"I appreciate the gifts."

"Right. Put the painting in the pad at Bayswater. Jesus."

He was still shaking his head when I left. Shop Street was hopping,

> mimes
> buskers
> fire-eaters

A guy was making models from bits of wire. Constructing amazing shapes in minutes. I asked him if he could make something specific. He said,

"Anything except money."

Five minutes later, he handed me the assignment. I gave him a few quid, said,

"You're really talented."

"Tell the Arts Council."

"In that day you shall begin to possess the solitude you have so long desired. Do not ask me when it will be or where or how. On a mountain or in a prison, in a desert or in a concentration camp. It does not matter. So, do not ask me because I am not going to tell you. You will not know until you are in it."

Thomas Merton, *The Seven Storey Mountain*

I went to the hospital and had the cast removed from my fingers. Looking at them, they seemed shrivelled, shrunken. The doctor gave me a small ball, said,

"Squeeze this firmly during the day, gradually restoring the strength."

The nurse was staring and I asked,

"What?"

"You'll be able to shave now."

I fingered my beard, asked,

"You don't like it?"

"Makes you look old."

"I feel old."

"Arrah, go on our that."

I thought I'd miss Irish nurses. I'd arranged to meet Cathy B. at Nestor's. She asked,

"Where?"

I gave the directions. The weather was holding and the sun cracked against my eyes.

In Nestor's, the sentry ignored me, so I figured my fame had ended. I took my hard chair and Jeff arrived with the coffee. I put my street purchase on the table. He said,

"Oh, wow!"

It was a miniature Harley, perfect in the small details. I said,

"It's my way of saying goodbye."

"You're leaving?"

"Yeah."
He didn't ask

> where
> when
> or even
> why.

Just nodded.
Cathy breezed in, looked round and said,
"What is this . . . a kitchen?"
"Welcome back, Mrs . . . what . . . ?"
"Mrs Disappointed."
"What?"
"Everett's gone. Met an American in Listowel and legged it."
"Jesus, I'm sorry."
"I'm not, he was a dick-head."
Jeff came over, said,
"Get you something."
"Spritzer."
I was tempted to join her. She watched Jeff walk away, said,
"Nice butt!"
"He's into bikes."
"My kinda guy."
He brought the drink and gave her a dazzling smile. I thought Jeff still had some moves. Cathy said,
"You old guys, you got class."
I laughed as if I meant it, said,
"I'm moving to London."
"Don't bother."
"What?"

"I'm from London . . . remember? Save yerself the trip."

"It's a done deal. I've bought the ticket."

"Whatever."

She took a sip, said,

"Perfect."

"I'm serious, Cathy, I'm off."

"The bar guy, is he married?"

"No . . . he used to be in a band."

"I'm in love."

"Cathy . . . yo . . . could we just focus for a minute here. Do you need money?"

"Naw, I've got gigs lined up."

I stood up, asked,

"Want to take a walk, feed the swans?"

"I'm gonna hang here a bit, put the make on this dude."

I was expecting a hug, would have settled for an air kiss, said,

"Well, see you then."

"Yeah, yeah, like later."

I squeezed the ball in my left hand. If it helped anything, I didn't notice.

STORMS

I had one hell of a bad dream. Like you see the guy in the movie, waking, drenched in sweat, shouting,

"Nam . . . incoming."

Like that.

I was dreaming of Padraig, Sean, Planter, Ford, Sarah Henderson. Lined up before me, eyes black in death, reaching for me. No matter how I ran, they were always in front of me. I was screaming,

"Leave me alone or I'll drink."

Came to with a shout. The sun was streaming through the windows, and I felt such dread as I had never known. Staggered outa bed and got a beta-b — fast. If I had known how to pray any more, I'd have gone for it. I said,

"Sé do bheatha, a Mhuire."

The opening of the Hail Mary in Irish. Began to ease. My early schooling had been solely through Irish. Moving up a grade, we had to relearn our prayers through English. During the transition period, I was prayerless.

Believed if I died, I'd go straight to hell. Those were the early nights of terror. As I got the swing of the new liturgy, the terror abated. Somewhere, though, the idea rooted that I'd been safer in Irish.

Serendipity was about to come calling. Coincidence being when God wants to maintain a low profile. When He's side-stepping the paparazzi.

I'd had my shower, managed a weak coffee and dressed. Wearing a faded-to-white denim shirt, tan needle cords, and the moks, I could have passed for an out of focus American Express ad.

Knock on the door. I hoped to hell it wasn't Sutton.

Janet.

She said,

"I hate to intrude."

"That's OK."

"Mrs Bailey said you're leaving."

"I am."

"I'd like you to have these."

She stretched out her hand. A black rosary beads. They appeared to shine. As I took them, they looked like handcuffs against the denim. She said,

"They were blessed at Knock."

"I am very moved, Janet. I'll keep them with me always."

She got shy and I added,

"I'll miss you."

A full blush. Not something you see too often any more so, to cover, I asked,

"Do you eat chocolate?"

"Oh God, I *love* it."

"Well, I'm going to get you a vulgar amount in a fancy box."

"With the dog on the lid?"

"Exactly."

She left with the blush in neon.

I put the beads under my pillow. I could use all the help available.

Walking towards the statue of Pádraig Ó Conaire, a garda approached me. I thought,

"Uh-dh."

He asked,

"Mr Taylor? Mr Jack Taylor?"

They call you mister, call a lawyer. I said,

"Yeah."

"Superintendent Clancy would like a word. This way."

He led the way to a black Daimler. The back door opened and a voice said,

"Get in, Jack."

I did.

Clancy was in full uniform. All the epaulettes, insignia on show. He was stouter than our previous meeting. I said,

"Not getting to the links too often?"

"What?"

"Golf. I hear you play with the big boys."

His face was purple, the eyes bulging. The guy used to be skinnier than a rat. He said,

"You should take it up, good for the health."

"I can't deny you're the living proof."

Shook his head, said,

"Always with the mouth, Jack."

The driver was built like the proverbial shithouse. Muscles bulging in his neck. Clancy said,

"I might owe you an apology."

"Might?"

"The suicides. Seems you were on to something."

"And, Super, are you on to something . . . like the whereabouts of Mr Planter?"

Clancy sighed, said,

"He's long gone. Money buys a lot of clout."

I didn't want to push too far in this direction, said,

"I'm leaving Galway."

"Indeed. Any hope your friend Sutton will go with you?"

"Don't think so. His muse is here."

Clancy was quiet, then,

"Did you know he once applied to the force?"

"Sutton?"

"Oh yes. Turned him down, there are standards."

"Are you sure? They took us."

He allowed himself a grim smile, said,

"You could have gone far."

"Wow, maybe even turned out like you."

He put out his hand. I was fascinated by his shoes. Heavy black jobs, with a shine you could see yourself in. I took his hand. He asked,

"Are you leaving because of Coffey?"

"What . . . who?"

"You remember him, a gombeen from Cork."

I let go his hand, pulled my eyes away from those shoes, said,

"Oh yeah, a big thick yoke. Fair hurler though."

"He works under me, and to hear him tell it, the Ann Henderson wan is working like a whore under him."

The words hung in the air. I could see the driver shift awkwardly behind the wheel. A line of sweat popped out along my brow. I could feel Clancy's grin in my

296

back. The world spun for a minute and I thought I'd fall. Must have been the sudden exposure to the sun. Took a second, then leant back into the car. With all my might I spat on those fine garda shoes.

I went into Supermacs on the square. Needed something very cold. Got a large Coke, ice-loaded, and took a window seat. My eyes were stinging, and I squeezed the ball in my left hand till my fingers ached. Took a long swallow of the Coke, felt the ice click against my teeth. A red cloud seemed to bend my vision. More Coke, then the sugar rush kicked.

It helped.

My vision cleared and I stopped the incessant squeezing. A man approached my table, said,

"Jack."

I looked up. Knew the face but couldn't place the name. He said,

"I'm Brendan Flood."

"Ah . . . the God guy."

"May I sit?"

"I'd prefer if you didn't, pal. I'm all out on guards."

"Ex-guards."

"Whatever."

"I need to tell you something."

"Is it about God again?"

"Everything's about God."

He sat and I looked out the window. Despite the sunshine, I could see black clouds on the horizon. Flood said,

"A storm is coming!"

"Are you being biblical or informative?"

"I heard it on the news."

I didn't answer, figured he'd spout some homily and be gone. How long could it take? He said,

"My condolences on the death of your friend Sean Grogan."

"Thanks."

"There is information."

"What?"

"On the car."

"Tell me."

"A yellow car."

"But there's a lot of those."

"Eye witnesses say it looked deliberate."

"Deliberate?"

"The guards interviewed the witnesses but they missed one. A boy of eleven, he collects number plates. He didn't get the actual digits but he did see a sticker."

He paused, then,

"It was CLFD."

"Clifden!"

He stood up, nodded at the approaching storm, said,

"God's intense displeasure."

I had shopping to do. Went to Holland's and got a mega box of chocolates. The cute dog on the lid. Next to the off-licence, and took some looking, but located a stone bottle of Dutch gin. Back to the hotel and left the chocolates at Reception. Mrs Bailey said,

"These are for Janet?"

"They are."

"She'll be delirious."

"Are we on for our nightcap tonight?"

"Lovely, around eleven?"

"Great."

NIMMO'S PIER

On the western shore of the Corrib, it stretches from the Claddagh Quay past Ringhanane Quay. Designed by Alexander Nimmo, it was built in 1822. The locals at the time were heavily opposed to it. Remained in use until the new commercial dock made it redundant in the early 1840s. The Claddagh Piers were repaired between 1843–51 and all had been linked to Nimmo's Pier by 1852.

****

Rats the size of domestic cats have been sighted on the eastern rim of the pier. They remain, as yet . . . un-christened.

Round seven in the evening, the heavens opened and rain lashed the city. Heavy and unrelenting. I lay on my bed and listened. My mind I kept blank and refused to ponder the endless possibilities.

At eleven, I went down to the bar, and Mrs Bailey was waiting. I'd worn my suit. She was all decked out, said,

"We're two dotes."

I'm sure it was a lovely evening. 'Cept, I don't remember it. My mind had moved to a place of ice, and Mrs Bailey talked for two. I do know she said,

"You're not touching the hard stuff."

"For now."

She didn't press. I watched the clock over the bar. When it got to two, Mrs Bailey said,

"I'll have to call it a night."

Her parting words:

"If you ever need a friend . . ."

Her hug near touched me but not enough.

I went to my room, looked out the window. If anything, the rain was heavier. I got my holdall and put the gin in. Next, I put on my guard's all-weather coat. Then I phoned Sutton, heard,

" 'Lo?"

"Sutton, it's Jack. You said you don't sleep much."

"Got that right."

"I need to see you."

"Sure . . . tomorrow . . . OK."

"Now! I have a bottle of gin."

"Ah, *now* you're talking. Where will I meet you?"

"Nimmo's Pier."

"What, there's a bloody gale out there."

"It's beautiful like that. Jeez, you're the artist, do I have to convince you?"

"Yeah, wild gin on a wild night. I love it."

"See you there."

Not a soul on the streets. As I got to Claddagh, the wind threatened to blow me over the quay. I could see the swans huddled against the boats.

When I got to Nimmo's, I leaned against the wall, watching the black bay. It was fiercely beautiful. A car's headlights turned at the football pitch, began to cruise down the pier. Reaching out, the lights illuminated me. I waved. The engine was turned off and Sutton opened the door. He had only a t-shirt and jeans, shouted at the night,

"I love it."

Fought against the wind to join me, said,

"Yah mad bastard, this was a great idea. Where's the booze?"

I unzipped the holdall, handed over the bottle. He said,

"Genever . . . mighty."

He took a huge swig and I asked,

"Do you remember the time we went to the dance in South Armagh?"

He lowered the bottle, said,

"Yeah . . ."

"A car followed us and I asked you which *side* they were on."

"Vaguely."

"You said the bad side, and I asked which one was that."

He nodded, I continued,

"You said the one that follows you at four in the morning."

He gave a gut laugh, most parts gin. I said,

"It's near four in the morning now, and you're the bad side."

"What?"

"You killed Sean. The Clifden tag on a yellow car, it was spotted."

He put the bottle down, considered, then,

"I did it for us."

"For us?"

His words came in a rush.

"One night, late . . . in Grogan's, I was pissed, trying to get a rise out of him. I told him we killed Ford."

"And you think Sean would have told!"

"Not then . . . but he hated me. The bastard took my painting down. Sooner or later he'd have made a call."

I said,

"Sutton."

And kneed him in the balls. Grabbed his t-shirt and dragged him towards the edge. He screamed,

"Jack . . . Jesus . . . I can't swim."

I waited a few moments, braced against the wind and said,

"I know that."

Threw him over. Picked up the stone bottle and smelled it. The power reached all the way to my toes. Reaching back, I threw high and long.

If there was a splash, I didn't hear it.

As I buttoned up against the wind, I remembered the time in the Newry pub. Sutton had grabbed "The Hound of Heaven" from me and said,

"Francis Thompson died roaring; it's how alkies die!"

I couldn't verify this. The wind was too loud.